PRAISE FOR TOM PHILBIN AND HIS PREVIOUS NOVELS

"As close to the real thing as I've ever read."

Frank Garrido, N.Y.P.D.
Undercover cop

"Grippingly real, outstanding."

John Carlton, N.Y.P.D.
Retired

"Great. These books read like they were written by a cop on the job."

Kenny Wilkinson, N.Y.P.D.
Retired

"Filled with mutts, maniacs and mayhem—just like I remember!"

Blake Williams, N.Y.P.D.
Retired

Also by Tom Philbin
Published by Fawcett Gold Medal Books:

THE YEARBOOK KILLERS
JAMAICA KILL
PRECINCT: SIBERIA
UNDER COVER
COP KILLER
A MATTER OF DEGREE
STREET KILLER
DEATH SENTENCE

THE PROSECUTOR

Tom Philbin

FAWCETT GOLD MEDAL • NEW YORK

A Fawcett Gold Medal Book
Published by Ballantine Books

Library of Congress Catalog Card Number: 90-93475
ISBN 0-449-14673-1

Manufactured in the United States of America

First Edition: March 1991

For Nick Gerlach

CHAPTER 1

Onofrio Racanelli, district attorney of Bronx County, was sitting at his desk in his office on the sixth floor of the Bronx County Courthouse, a massive gray concrete structure on the Grand Concourse and 158th Street.

Racanelli glanced at his watch. It was 10:02 P.M. He would handle one more piece of paper, then leave. He had been in the office, as usual, since 6:45 A.M.

He picked up a press release from his IN box. Stapled to the release were newspaper reports on the crime and a copy of the indictment. The package, by helping reporters do their stories, would elicit warmer feelings on their part toward the DA's office. New York City reporters were probably the toughest in the world. But they were also human, and Racanelli schmoozed them in any way he could. Ultimately he answered to the people who had elected him, but people were swayed by what they read in the papers and watched on TV. There were very few people who thought for themselves.

He read, as usual, very slowly. It was important that releases not offend anyone and that the facts be carefully stated so that the suspect's rights were not abridged.

This was the story of a thirty-seven-year-old male Hispanic named Juan Gonzalez, who had gotten drunk, then driven his rented car into a bunch of kids crossing Southern Boulevard. The result was that a nine-year-old black girl named Mercedes Briggs had been killed. An eight-year-old boy named Tod Raymonds had been struck by a toppled lamppole and had been in intensive care for fifteen days. He was now in a coma and living on a respirator. A third kid had suffered severe facial lacerations, two broken thigh bones, and a fractured spleen. He was in the best condition of all.

Racanelli finished the piece, but then fixed on one of his quotes:

"Gonzalez's behavior while driving the car that killed one child and critically injured two others, clearly demonstrated a depraved disregard for human life."

It was true, Racanelli thought. Gonzalez had two priors, both DWIs. Racanelli had assigned Laura Lucarelli to the case. She was one of the most competent—and tough—people he had, and he had instructed her to max it out, not to plead it down, no matter what. This guy was going to jail.

He put his small, neat initials on the release and placed it on a massive pile on the OUT box. The IN box was practically empty. He stood up and stretched.

Even after such a long day he felt good. He was six feet tall, kept his weight down to 165, and only ate healthy foods that translated into energy.

He went over to a closet door, opened it, took out his dark, well-pressed jacket, and put it on.

Then he looked at himself in a long mirror on the back of the door. He adjusted his jacket a little so it lay flatter against his shoulders. He checked his shoes, no scuffs or dullness, and ran a hand over his neatly combed, short dark hair.

He went back to the desk, picked up the phone, and punched out a three-digit extension.

"Ready, Jack," he said to Jack Willis, one of a detail of N.Y.P.D. detectives who guarded him.

"Yes, sir. See you downstairs?"

"Two minutes."

* * *

Five minutes later, Racanelli was sitting in the back of an armored black sedan. Willis was driving, and another detective, Larsen, was sitting beside him in the passenger seat.

The routes to his home were varied so they could spot anyone who might be following them. Tonight, they took the Concourse.

Racanelli glanced idly out of the windows as they went along. A light, cold rain was falling. It was mid-October, and it occurred to him that the leaves would soon be turning. When winter came, there would be less crime. The only thing that could cut down on cocaine dealing was the cold.

His route up the Concourse was flanked by large, elegant apartment buildings, some of which had awnings, remnants from another time when the eight-lane Concourse was the place where rich people lived.

Now the buildings were filled with crime scenes—warm and homey apartments where families once lived had turned into places where drugs were sold, where people were shot or knifed, where blood oozed out into the squalor the victims lived in.

Most of the Bronx was like this. Once it had been almost like a country town where everybody knew everybody else. It had been a great place to grow up. Now, people had fled to the suburbs. Racanelli could remember when the Bronx phone book was two inches thick. Today it was about a half inch.

One thing Racanelli knew: he was not leaving. He had been district attorney for five years and, during that time, private interests had made him offers that would have made him rich—for life.

But he hadn't accepted and never would. He was proud of being in public service, and he demanded that same pride from the 213 people who worked for him.

"The best thing you can do in your life," he would tell

new ADAs, "is help other people. And one way to do that is by making sure that everyone in society lives by the rule of law. As a prosecutor you will be feared and hated . . . but just remember that without prosecutors laws are meaningless, and laws are the glue that holds society together."

Some new ADAs would invariably find it hard to believe that Racanelli could believe such high-sounding stuff. Wasn't he a district attorney because, one day, he could use the position as a launching pad to higher things?

Those who knew him well knew the answer to that. Racanelli believed in what he was doing.

Racanelli lived in an ordinary old frame house—two stories, gingerbread trim, small front yard surrounded by wrought-iron fence—that he had been raised in. The fact that it was the Arthur Avenue section was ironic. The neighborhood teemed with wise guys and relatives of wise guys. Racanelli had put quite a few wise guys in jail. It was like the mongeese and cobras living together, but, somehow, he and the wise guys were able to section off their lives: the neighborhood was not the arena where they fought each other—possibly to the death.

But Racanelli had no warm feelings toward them, no feelings of bemused tolerance colored by the Damon Runyon–like attitude of the media. Racanelli hated the Mafia. They were vicious, homicidal thugs who worked constantly to tear apart the fabric of society. Never mind, too, that the Mafia was Italian and besmirched the ethnicity of all Italians.

He knew, too, that the Mafia hated and feared him. They had good reason. He had succeeded in putting twenty-three Mafiosi away for long prison terms, and they knew he was working to put others away. And that once he got an indictment the charged person was in deep trouble because Racanelli rarely, if ever, went into court without the goods.

When he got home, his mother, Angelina, was already in bed. She slept in a bedroom upstairs that she had once shared with his father, Luigi. Indeed, everything in the room, except for Pop's clothing, which she had taken a long time to give away, was the same as it had been when he was alive.

He climbed the stairs and went down the hall. The door was open. He looked in.

A night-light was on, and he could see her head on the pillow, facing away from him. He saw what he wanted to see: the rhythmic rising of her chest.

He felt better; some small tension in him eased.

He went downstairs to the kitchen to get an apple. His mother had left him a note on the refrigerator.

Dear Ono,
Something in the refrigerator for you.
Love,
Mama

What was in the refrigerator for him was a cannoli, an Italian confection that contained perhaps twelve thousand calories. Italian mamas were wise, but they would never understand what it meant to diet.

He went into the foyer, where he had left the walkie-talkie, and did what he always did when Mama left something like this for him. He activated it. Larsen responded.

"Ray," he said into the device, "got something here for your arteries."

"Super. Be right there."

In bed, Racanelli read for a while—a case file—then turned off the light, and drifted off to sleep.

The ringing phone awakened him.

He glanced at the clock radio—2:03—and picked up. It was either a wrong number or something important. Very few people had his home number.

"Yes?"

"Oh, yes sir, Mr. Racanelli. Herb Maher. Sorry to call you at home . . ."

Herb Maher was a relatively new ADA assigned to homicide duty. For the twenty-four hours he was on duty, he would catch any homicide that occurred. He would keep the case if it was simple enough, or it would be assigned to a more experienced ADA.

". . . but," Maher continued, "a woman's been murdered and I . . . uh . . . think you know her. I remember she was in your office a few months ago."

"Who?"

"Irmgard Werner?"

Racanelli didn't miss a beat.

"How do you know it's her?"

"She was found in her apartment in the Hotel Miramar. The super says it's her."

"What happened?" Racanelli asked.

"Apparently she was stabbed."

"When?"

"We don't know. The ME's on his way."

"Detectives there?"

"No. Just cops . . . Uh . . . uniformed police."

"Put a lid on the scene," Racanelli said. "You're the chief law enforcement official there. I don't want anything touched by anyone except detectives."

"Yes, sir."

Racanelli made one call—to Joe Lawless. Most people thought that detectives were competent—Sherlock Holmes in Robert Hall suits. But most were incompetent and careless and only cared about their pay and pensions.

Joe Lawless was a good one. He was Felony Squad commander at the Five Three—Fort Siberia—and a tough, hard, dedicated investigator who got results.

Racanelli wanted Lawless on this one.

He got through to Lawless and explained briefly what had happened. Lawless, who lived on Pelham Bay Parkway, said he would leave for the scene immediately, that he would be there in fifteen minutes.

Then Racanelli started to get dressed and tried to focus on who he would assign to the case.

Then, for just a moment, his throat thickened.

Goddammit, he thought, Goddammit. Why her?

Chapter 2

It was raining as Racanelli and the two detectives tooled across Fordham Road.

He was thinking about Irmgard Werner.

He had first met her about a year ago, when he was in the process of prosecuting Ling Dang Pran, a sixty-three-year-old Vietnamese slumlord who operated a number of welfare hotels for the city.

Pran's four buildings had been hit by building inspectors with thousands of sanitary and safety violations, but he had done nothing to bring the buildings into compliance.

About two years before, Racanelli had decided to make Pran a priority and an example to other slum landlords. To take him down hard and put him in jail.

But it was not easy.

While they had innumerable physical violations against

Pran, they did not have witnesses—people who could testify about the various deprivations they suffered. Investigators discovered that the tenants were reluctant to talk about what it was like to go without heat and hot water and worry about rats crawling out of a wall to bite you or your children.

People were simply afraid. The six-by-eight rat hole for which the city paid Pran a thousand dollars a month beat the street, where they feared they might end up if they testified against him.

Then, when Racanelli was close to shelving the case, probably forever, Irmgard Werner had called. She told him that she would testify against Pran. Optimistic—though guarded—he made an appointment to see her.

He remembered his first view of her. Thin, gray hair, hand-me-down clothes, an obvious alcoholic, or ex-alcoholic, or maybe on drugs.

His immediate impression was one of weakness and flakiness.

Irmgard seemed to sense his feelings. She said that she would testify, and she thought she would be a good witness.

"I'm glad," Racanelli had said, "but I wonder why you're doing it."

She told him a little story.

"People who drink," she said, "can usually only come back—if they ever come back—when they bottom out. I bottomed out in a mental hospital in Baltimore. I just woke up there in this gray ward with my body covered with sores and welts, my eyes swollen, and I was shaking terribly. They gave me a sedative, but even that didn't help. I knew I was going to die.

"And then," she continued, "just when I knew my life was starting to ebb away, I felt Jesus in the ward with me. I felt his love. He held out his arms and took me in them and told me that with his love I would make it back. From that moment to this I have not had a drink . . . .

"Let's just say," she continued, "that I want to see how much courage I have. If I could beat the bottle, I figure I can beat my fear of Pran. Jesus will be at my side."

Racanelli was impressed. As sophisticated as he was, he knew the power of faith, and he knew the power of Jesus. Indeed, he himself started every day of his life with mass at Our Lady Queen of Sorrows.

For about ten days before the trial, Racanelli met with Irmgard almost every day to counsel her on what to expect in court, and to clarify and articulate her testimony. A trial was nothing if not two Broadway shows, with the defense attorney and prosecutor directing their respective casts. The truth was almost incidental.

She was very smart and had a good memory, but deep inside, despite his own faith in the power of faith, he harbored doubts about her ability to stand up in court. You looked in her face and you could see years of not showing up, of broken promises, of dreams that had died. You saw someone who had been reduced to animal instincts. You wondered what was left inside. Was there enough to stand up to the brutal process of cross-examination, which could cut to the essence of a person?

He remembered calling her to the stand and her thin figure moving slowly but with great dignity toward it. To Racanelli, it was a moment of transcendent courage, and he desperately wanted to win the case—not just because it was the right thing, that it would make things better for tenants everywhere, but he wanted to win it for her.

On direct, she testified well, and then he gave her up to Pran's attorney, a three-hundred-dollar-an-hour man named Leonard Sims who was, by turns, unctuous and abusive. Looking over the trial transcript months later, Racanelli counted that he had objected during Sims's cross fifty-three times.

In sum, Sims came at Irmgard Werner with a withering ferocity. He did cut to her essence, and she was undaunted. Three hours after he had started on her, Sims walked away, he was the one who had been broken—by his own inability to take Irmgard apart.

The jury was out a half hour, and it convicted Pran on every single charge against him.

Later, Racanelli got to know Irmgard Werner a lot better. She would call him from time to time, and he would call her, and they met for lunch three or four times; once in the office cafeteria.

She had had an incredible amount of heartbreak in her life; her 12-year-old son had drowned at a picnic, she had lost a baby to sudden infant death syndrome, her husband had run away with someone else at a time when she was pregnant and had no means of support except him.

She had started to drink, and that compounded the problems. Eventually the state took away her only child, Rebecca, and put her in a foster home.

How strange people are, he had thought. You can assume they are dead, but somehow they survive.

Racanelli had discovered that Irmgard had a master's degree in English, had taught American Literature on the college level, and one day thought she might want to even try to go back to teaching.

After that day on the stand, he would never doubt what Irmgard Werner was capable of.

She had called him just a month ago.

"I'm doing very well, Ono. I'm getting really reacquainted with my daughter and, maybe, someone else. . . ."

"Really? Who's that?"

But she said it was a little premature to talk about anything.

And now she was dead. Just another stat, one of the five murders committed every day in New York City.

Racanelli felt an emptiness growing inside him, but he thought it away, and put on his professional mask as the Hotel Miramar came into view.

CHAPTER 3

The Hotel Miramar was a huge, fancy, white-brick structure on the corner of 178th Street and the Concourse. It was only ten minutes by cab or subway from Yankee Stadium, and had been a favorite spot for out-of-towners.

But that was many years ago. Today it was a welfare hotel, its once elegant, spacious rooms divided into the tiny cubicles the city paid so dearly for.

The detectives dropped Racanelli off at the front entrance. A small crowd, most of them under a tattered awning, were clustered on both sides of the entrance. A uniformed cop was monitoring who went in and out.

There were two blue-and-whites and the wagon from the morgue.

Racanelli showed his ID to the patrolman and went into the lobby.

The lobby was large, and also bore signs of how elegant the building once had been. There were fancy moldings on walls and ceilings beneath faded paint, and in the ceiling was a large rosette that had once housed an elegant chandelier. It now contained fluorescent lights.

It all struck Racanelli as very sad.

Two dimly lit halls led off the lobby. Racanelli blinked. Crime scene tape blocked off the hall that, he knew, led to Irmgard's apartment.

Reluctantly, though it didn't show on his face, he moved toward the hall. He showed his ID to the cop there, then went down the hall to Irmgard's room.

The door was open. He stood in the doorway.

The room was a mess, things scattered all over, but he didn't get a chance to look too hard. The bed drew his eyes like iron filings to a magnet.

The mattress was half off the bed and was covered by a white bedspread spattered with bright red blood.

He pulled his eyes away and scanned the room. There was a guy taking fingerprints off a windowsill; the window was open.

Another guy was photographing the room.

Lawless and Maher were standing on the far side of the bed, which was in the middle of the room, parallel to the wall the door was on. They were looking down.

Someone was kneeling down. Racanelli recognized the balding head of Vic Onairuts, the medical examiner.

Lawless waved him in, answering the question in Racanelli's mind of whether it was all right. He picked his way through the stuff scattered on the floor, came to the far side of the bed, and looked down.

Hope soared.

It did not look like Irmgard. He had not seen her in awhile, but this did not look like her!

The fully dressed woman was on her stomach, her face on its left side, hands down at her side.

No, it definitely did not look like her.

Irmgard was thin. This woman weighed more.

Irmgard's hair was gray and long; this woman's hair was short and blonde.

Heart hammering, something in him soaring, he got close to the face and looked.

The air went out of him.

The face was heavily made up, but the features were

unmistakable, and the light blue eyes, which were open, confirmed it.

"It's her," Racanelli said.

"Sorry," Lawless said.

"Yes, sir," Maher said, "sorry."

"What have you got?" Racanelli asked.

"Looks like a robbery," Lawless said. "The perp gained access through the window, which lets on to an alley."

"How'd she die?"

"Throat cut, stabbed in the chest," Onairuts said. "But she fought. She's got a couple of defensive wounds on her left hand."

"Also, Ono," Lawless said, "there are spatters at various points across the floor and on the wall. In other words, she was fighting and bleeding at the same time, so it was dispersed."

"How long has she been dead?"

"A couple of hours. She's still warm." Onairuts said, but then quickly looked up, his eyes sorrowful. He had realized that the description would rip at someone who knew the victim.

"I'm sorry to be so graphic."

"That's okay," Racanelli said. "Was she raped?"

"I don't know yet," Onairuts said.

"How did the perp exit?"

"Front door probably," Lawless said. "It was open. That's how she was discovered. A tenant next door saw the door open an inch or so and looked in."

"Any witnesses?" Racanelli asked.

"We don't know yet."

"I'd like you to handle this personally, Joe," Racanelli said. "I can clear it with Bledsoe."

Bledsoe was Captain Bledsoe, CO of the Five Three.

"You don't have to," Lawless said. "I was first here, so it's my squeal. Bledsoe wouldn't care anyway," Lawless said. "This isn't the kind of squeal that will get his name in the paper in a positive way."

Racanelli silently confirmed that. Bledsoe was a very self-serving man.

"I'd like to get the post done quickly," Racanelli said. "When can you do it, Vic?"

Onairuts looked up.

"Tomorrow morning, first thing."

"Okay."

Racanelli wanted to probe the room, but he knew he should wait until forensics was finished. Not that he could see much more. The room was so small you could practically touch all the walls at once.

He looked around from a stationary position, slowly turning his head this way and that.

Holy pictures dominated the walls, which were full of cracks and holes and hadn't been painted in many years.

There was a painting of Jesus, and of the Blessed Virgin, and The Holy Family, and St. Jude, Patron Saint of Impossible Causes. Irmgard had an impish sense of humor and once told Racanelli that Jesus was good, but in her case "it didn't hurt to back him up with Saint Jude."

And, yes, there was blood on the walls, long tear-drop-shaped spatters. He stopped looking at them.

An hour later, Racanelli was back in bed. He figured he'd better get a couple of hours more sleep.

Not all the evidence was in, but it did seem as if Irmgard was the victim of a robbery; somebody was searching for something. God knew what she had that was valuable enough to steal.

But he wondered. There were three locks on the door, including a Fox lock, but nothing to speak of on the window. That had, from what they could determine, been compromised with a knife.

Maybe it wasn't a random killing. Maybe it was one set up to look this way.

By Pran. A revenge killing. Pran knew lots of people who would kill for a song. He would check that out. They would check a lot of things out.

Racanelli shifted in the bed, trying to get into a position where he could sleep. He could hear rain gurgling in the gutters.

Twenty minutes later, he was still very much awake. He kept thinking about Irmgard, various images from various times, and then, one special scene. . . .

It was that day in court when they came in with the guilty verdict against Pran.

In the soft chaos that rippled through the court, he had turned around and found Irmgard's face in the crowd and had smiled, and she had smiled back. It was a smile he would never forget, for in that moment it seemed to transform her face, make it a different face, a beautiful, happy face that had never known any pain. She had smiled from deep inside her heart. And so did he because, at that moment, he was acutely aware of how what he was doing with his life mattered very much. He was making a difference for that face in the crowd, all the faces in the crowd.

Goddammit.

CHAPTER 4

For Frank Piccolo, it was almost like old times.

It was a Friday morning, about eleven o'clock, and he was sitting in the kitchen of his four-room apartment on Bainbridge Avenue in the Bronx. He was sipping some cold guinea red, and dust glittered in the sun, which was streaming through the window in thick, warm bars. Behind him he would hear the occasional gentle stirring of one or more of the pets he kept in cages or cases in the living room down the hall. They were the boa, the monitor lizard, the python, and the Tasmanian devil.

Most important, sitting across the table from him, also sipping wine, was his "new" partner and roommate, Howie Stein. They had been together two years now, and during that time Piccolo had drawn closer to him than anyone, except his deceased partner Eddie Edmunton.

Howie was some piece of work. Frank figured himself very lucky to have him as a partner. Some cops at the Five Three, where Frank was a detective, would say that Frank was lucky to have any partner.

Most guys wouldn't work with him because they were afraid of either getting in trouble with the brass or getting killed. The Five Three—Precinct Siberia—was punishment duty, the place where misfit cops were sent. It was a really dangerous place to work. With a partner like Piccolo it could be like walking through a fire carrying an open can of gas.

But Stein was not only willing to serve with Piccolo, he liked it.

Stein himself was considered a high-risk persona by most cops. He had almost been thrown off the job a number of times, as had Piccolo, and had been involved in a very nasty shoot-out in the Harlem tenement where, when the smoke cleared, three drug dealers and a cop had been killed. Stein's judgment had been seriously questioned by the shooting board that was convened.

In Stein's personnel jacket there were various incidents—such as punching out his CO—that indicated he was mentally unstable.

Piccolo's jacket was chockful of brutality complaints. Only three other people in the department had more. One was in a mental institution, one was in jail, and the third was in the boneyard as a result of having eaten his .38 one day.

In fact, the only thing that had saved either man was their work on the street. Individually and collectively they had made innumerable felony collars and had been cited many times for outstanding police work. It was hard to justify firing cops with their records, and any CO who they had been working for came to realize that their efforts could greatly increase clearance numbers.

Piccolo took another sip of the wine and looked at Stein.

They made some pair, Piccolo thought. Opposite in a lot of ways.

Their looks, for one thing.

Piccolo was short, big-nosed, black-haired, and often walked the streets without his teeth. His toothless smile made him look exactly what he was: nuts.

Howie had a shock of carrot-red hair and freckles and deep-set deep brown eyes. He was nice-looking and had all his teeth. Except there was a certain glitter that also marked him as crazy. "You look in them eyes," one brother cop had said, "you see nothing but Barnum and Bailey."

Piccolo was short and thin. Howie was tall and muscular

and had a left arm—developed from years of one-armed pulling of dumbwaiters in the Bronx where he was raised—that was twice as thick as his right arm and twice as hairy. It featured thick, ropelike veins and almost seemed separate from his body. His nickname was "Thunderfist." Piccolo had seen him punch people out and had told him once that he thought Howie could KO a charging rhino with a single punch.

Howie was a thinker and Piccolo was not.

Howie had been raised a Jew and Piccolo a Catholic, though both men were nonreligious now.

Piccolo smiled broadly.

"What are you smiling at?" Howie asked.

"Our street name. Pisser."

"Oh, yeah." Howie smiled.

The nickname, given to them by a drug dealer, was "Frankenstein" after Frank and Stein, but mostly after the feeling they evoked when they appeared. Terror.

Indeed.

Piccolo smiled again. When Frankenstein came down any block in Siberia it cleared, like roaches when you turn the light on in the kitchen in the middle of night.

The bad guys knew what they were like. Crazed. Ruthless. Anything goes. "Like Dirty Harry, but without his compassion," as one cop said.

Taking out drug dealers was their specialty.

They knew who the dealers and users were, and paid them equal respect: zero. If Frankenstein was on tour and they suspected you of dealing but couldn't prove it, they would merely beat the shit out of you. If they caught you carrying, they would beat the shit out of you and arrest you. If they knew you were a chronic dealer but couldn't prove it, they would beat the shit out of you, plant some weight, and then arrest you.

The planted evidence had seen so much duty that at one

point the property clerk took Piccolo aside and warned him to change the package. "It looks like it's been through World War Two," he said.

Piccolo did not deep-think such actions. To him, it was war, and that's the way you played it.

As a thinker, Stein did, but he chose as he put it "to take a pragmatic stance." He didn't want to end up "another Neville Chamberlain."

So his thunderfist was constantly in motion.

Many dealers took special care to avoid Frankenstein. Among other things, some would pay a lookout to watch for them. To deal with this, Frankenstein developed sly approaches. Once they used a limo. When the dealers saw the big, sleek, black Lincoln Town Car moving down the block they wondered what heavy hitter was in it. They saw too late that the driver with the black suit and black cap was Frank Piccolo . . . and his spiffily dressed passenger was Stein. Frankenstein cuffed 'em all and then, because it deeply affected the funny bone of both men, drove their collars to the station in the limousine.

A number of dealers wanted to whack Frankenstein, but there were three things going against this.

When the young cop named Byrne had been whacked in Jamaica, the bad guys had noted how nasty and determined cops could be when one of their own was put down.

Second, they had learned that anybody will flip on anybody to save their ass. Who could they commission for the hit without risking a flip—and prosecution—later?

Third, there was the Frankenstein "code." They made it known that if either of them got whacked the other would pursue the perp or perps to the death. Stein did not yet have a reputation in Siberia, but Piccolo did. Everyone knew he had murdered the Jamaican who had gunned down his partner—and no one had any doubt about what Stein would do. He would not be Piccolo's partner if he couldn't do it.

Piccolo topped off his water glass and for a fleeting moment thought of what life would be like without Howie. His stomach went hollow, and for an excruciating moment he remembered the day he learned about Eddie being gunned down.

He did not even want to think about losing Howie. When Eddie got killed he almost didn't make it. Joe Lawless and the other squad guys had nursed him through. Even his ex-wife had been kind, and it helped when he was able to shoot the shooter.

Piccolo took a slug of the wine. The thought went away.

"So how you doing, buddy?" Piccolo asked.

"Fine," Stein said. "You ever read Nietzsche?"

Piccolo's brow furrowed.

"Who's that? He play linebacker for the Packers?"

"No. Philosopher."

"The only philosopher I ever knew was my father. He told me I thought about girls too much and I should stop pulling my pud."

Stein nodded.

"I never talked to my father. He was a hard guy. Baker. My mother said that made him bitter about life. Having to get up in the middle of the night. But it went much deeper than that."

"My father was an electrician. And he had a fucking drinking problem. Can you imagine that? A drunken electrician? I think he burned down two fucking houses and a small skyscraper."

Stein chuckled. He took a delicate sip of the wine.

"Getting to like that wop wine, huh?" Piccolo said.

Stein nodded. But he didn't like it that much. He only drank it because Piccolo insisted.

"I never drank before I met you," he said, "particularly"—he glanced at an electric clock on the wall—"at eleven o'clock in the morning."

Piccolo smiled. He had his bridge out, and his eyes glittered.

"Look what you were missing," he said.

Stein nodded.

"Nietzsche had a very dark view of life. So did Schopenhauer."

"He played for the Lions, right?" Piccolo said.

"No, another philosopher. He was a four-foot hunchback. Loved beautiful women, but no one would love him back."

"No wonder the motherfucker was depressed," Piccolo said. "You think Tom Cruise is depressed? Fuck no. He's got looks, money, half the women in the country creaming in their jeans over him."

"Sometimes," Stein said, "I look on life like Nietzsche. Or I sometimes feel like Schopenhauer."

He was going to add that he also sometimes thought that their relationship would end violently, that one of them would be killed, but he knew it was a tender subject with Frank. He demurred.

Piccolo paused, reflective.

"I took a lot of shit when I was young," he said, "'cause I was short and ugly."

"You're not ugly," Stein said. "You know I took a lot of guff because I was a Jew in a Catholic neighborhood. All the Catholic kids hated Jews, said we killed Christ. Absurd. People build their value systems on stupidities, accidents of birth."

"Christ, you got some brain, you know that, Howie?"

"I always felt stupid. My father always said I was stupid."

"Yeah, my father was always holier than thou. Until one day my younger sister caught him fucking my aunt. One day that fucker left my mother and never came back."

His eyes misted.

"I believe in violence," Piccolo said. "That solves a lot of problems."

"Short term. Ultimately it is self-defeating. I mean I know we need it as cops, but someday maybe we'll live in a world where it's not necessary."

"Solved your problems, though, right?"

"You mean when I was a kid?"

"Yeah," Piccolo said, smiling broadly and taking another slug of the wine. "Where you had five fights in a row when you first moved into the neighborhood—and then only one years later because the dumb fuck didn't hear about the first five!"

Piccolo cackled, Stein tittered. For a big guy he had a high, insane laugh. It articulated a large part of his true personality.

Then for a moment, there was a silence.

"Good partners," Piccolo said, "are hard to find. I had a good one in Eddie . . . I got a good one now. . . ."

He gulped and stopped talking.

"Do you mind if I smoke?" Piccolo asked.

"No," Stein said. He didn't like it, but there were times when he wouldn't object. Frank needed a cigarette.

Piccolo lit an unfiltered Camel, dragged deeply. The smoke tumbled in the sunlight.

Howie knew what Piccolo was thinking.

"Hey, Frank," he said, "nothing's going to happen to either of us. We'll be all right."

Piccolo looked at him and said nothing.

By two o'clock, the wine bottle was empty and Piccolo was lying on the living room couch, lulled to sleep by the gentle stirrings of his pets.

Stein was in their bedroom reading an obscure medieval philosopher named Robert Grosstest.

The phone on the night table rang. Stein picked up.

"Hello."

"Is Frank there? This is Eddie Boyle."

"Just a minute, please."

Stein went in and roused Piccolo. He took the call in the kitchen.

"How's it going, Eddie?" Piccolo asked, but once he had heard the name he was totally awake—and tense. Eddie Boyle was a cop in Philly. There was one likely reason he called.

"Okay. Listen. I think we found the Ferret."

Fuck.

"Where?"

"Schuylkill River. Shot. We got him at the ME's office. Can you come down to ID him?"

"Yeah. I'll come down now."

They said good-bye. He hung up. Stein was staring at him.

"What's up?"

"They found the Ferret in the river. I got to go to the morgue to make him."

"Too bad, Frank," Stein said. "I'm sorry."

"Yeah," Piccolo said, "yeah."

"I'm going with you."

Piccolo nodded.

"I'll call Lawless, shift the tours," Piccolo said.

As he punched out the number, he said softly but with a voice filled with loathing:

"Motherfucker. Fat guinea scumbag motherfucker."

Stein knew he was referring to Angelo Capezzi, *capo di tutti di,* capi of the Philadelphia wise guys.

Chapter 5

Within two hours of the call from Eddie Boyle, Frankenstein was in Piccolo's black Trans Am halfway down the Jersey Turnpike on the way to Philadelphia. Massive clouds were bulked up on the horizon and were tinged peach, pink, and purple. Gorgeous. Piccolo didn't notice. He was thinking about the Ferret.

Piccolo had liked August "the Ferret" Rondolpho for a number of reasons, even though he was a pigeon, the lowest of the low in the criminal hierarchy. Piccolo and the Ferret had a lot in common. Both were small and dark and had black hair. Both had big liquid eyes and large noses.

Both were of Italian descent. Both were pretty sharp dressers.

And the Ferret could be trusted. His information was always aces. What he told you, you could take to the bank.

And he never tried to con Piccolo, a perilous undertaking at best.

But the thing Piccolo admired most was the Ferret's balls. True he was a snitch, but he took chances. Big chances. He had cast brass, dirigible-size stones. He would go into situations where no other snitch would tread. He would wear a wire in situations where most cops, even with full backup, would not.

The Ferret was unique.

Howie had met the Ferret when he and Piccolo were stinging Capezzi. The Ferret got along real well with Howie. The

Ferret was a thinker like Howie, and they would talk about books and shit that Piccolo never heard of. He was happy to see they got along.

Piccolo, who was driving, opened the driver's side window a couple of inches, then lit a cigarette with the car lighter. Howie didn't object. Like before, he knew that Piccolo was going through something bad now and needed his cigarettes.

Piccolo took a deep drag.

It all started when his nephew came and told him that someone had glommed his eighteen-wheeler. Frankenstein traced the theft to a Capezzi chop shop ring in Philly, then decided to sting Capezzi as well as get the nephew's truck back.

They worked up a plan, but it all depended on getting inside Capezzi's organization.

The Ferret, he knew, had not liked the Capezzi sting from the start. That's what his instincts told him, and he had great instincts.

The Ferret was afraid of Capezzi's slickness.

"He could find me out, Frank," the Ferret had told Piccolo when Piccolo first laid the proposal out.

Piccolo pooh-poohed this and said he would make it well worth the Ferret's while.

"It's worth five large," Piccolo said. "That's what you'll get."

The Ferret didn't ask where Piccolo was going to get the five large, but he knew he would get it. Piccolo was a man of his word.

Piccolo knew. He would get that much and more from stealing New York wise guy cars and selling them to their fellow wise guys in Philly. Neat.

There was also the pressure applied by Piccolo. It was hard to resist.

Reluctantly the Ferret did the job. He got Piccolo a

sit down with Vito Capezzi, the fat man's nephew, and he had been able to help locate the warehouse where the chop shop was housed, where they were cutting up not only eighteen-wheelers, but all kinds of other vehicles as well.

One day a joint task force swept into place and the result was a basket full of indictments.

They weren't able to connect any of it to Capezzi, but there was always the possibility they might. When you are trying to take down someone that high up in the family, about the only shot you have is for someone to flip. Though the indictments did not involve super heavy time, there were a number of perps collared who were three-time losers, and one or more might yet roll over.

That hadn't happened yet, and Piccolo doubted that it would. And just before they hit the chop shop the Ferret had disappeared, and no one was able to find him.

Frankenstein knew it was the worst when the Ferret didn't show up to claim his five large.

Piccolo flipped the cigarette out the window. He had the urge for another but resisted.

He glanced across at Howie.

"I was hoping against hope," he said.

Howie said nothing.

"The thing is," Piccolo said, "It's my fault. . . . He didn't want to do it. I made him. And for what? They closed down Capezzi's chop shop, but so far that fuck is breathing free air."

Howie looked at him.

"It's part of the grand design," he said. "Everything is preordained. In the stars, Frank. We don't know what's going to be, but things have been decided. By God, an infinite presence. There's nothing we can do about it."

There, Piccolo thought, Howie is talking some kind of horseshit he didn't understand, but he was trying to help. The thing was it didn't help. Nothing could help.

Cops say that the worst-looking corpse, even worse than what you get in an airline crash, is the "floater," a body that has been submerged in the water awhile. And the longer it's been down, the worse it looks.

Even if the crabs and fish don't get to it, anaerobic bacteria start to multiply after death, and they emit gases that swell the body up to half again as big as it was in life.

The skin turns white as a fish's belly, and takes on the texture they call "washerwoman's skin." If it's in salt water, the eyes will fall out, assuming the marine life doesn't get to them first.

Maybe it is worst because it still resembles a human being. In an airline crash bodies are often macerated and burned beyond recognition; they don't look human.

In the summer, the body blows up within a few days because the bacteria breed quickly in warmth. The gases make the body buoyant, and it will come up quickly or not at all, depending on what is secured to it. Cops say that to keep the average body down, some nine hundred pounds of weight must be on it.

In the winter, the gases build up slowly and the body takes a long time to come up, if it comes up at all.

Of course, in either case, summer or winter, the body will never come up if the gases are expelled, as sometimes happens when marine life eat through the abdomen, bleeding off the gases.

The nude body on the gurney in the Philadelphia morgue looked human, but very little like the Ferret.

Frankenstein, who were viewing it along with Boyle and an assistant ME, could recognize it because of a distinctive gold earring the Ferret always wore in his left ear. It was there.

"That's him," Piccolo said to the ME, whose name was Jenkins.

"You want a copy of the post?" Jenkins asked.

"Yeah," Piccolo said. "What's the deal?"

"Two shots in the back of the head with a .22."

Piccolo nodded. Standard wise guy clip.

"He was weighted down," Jenkins said, "with the transmission from a 1978 Pontiac."

Jenkins paused, then continued.

"He was tortured, too," he said.

"How?" Piccolo said. He had noticed various darkish patches all over the body.

"Stun gun, I think. You look close and you can see the twin burn marks."

Frankenstein stayed a few more minutes just looking at the body. Before they left, Piccolo touched one of the hands—it was ice cold—and nodded.

As they walked out of the building onto the street, Howie made no attempt to talk with Piccolo. He knew he couldn't. The little man was living inside his skull.

Anyway, Howie didn't feel like it. All he could think about was hurting somebody—bad.

CHAPTER 6

It was around two o'clock, the afternoon after the body of Irmgard Werner had been discovered. Racanelli was driving his blue Ford sedan south on the New Jersey Turnpike, and the scene there matched his mood, which was dark. He was moving through some of the ugliest country he had ever seen.

It looked like the back of an old radio, in King Kong scale. There were gas tanks, oil tanks, chemical tanks, odd-looking erector set structures clustered together. Smoke stacks emitted God knew what. And, occasionally, Racanelli would see dead-looking pools of water, tinted fuchsia or some other color not normally found in nature. He could not imagine what was in them.

He had the car windows shut, but occasionally he would get a whiff of something foul or acrid.

In a way, he thought, it was like driving through one long crime scene.

The land, he knew, had been figuratively gang raped. The assault had been long and leisurely, but the cumulative effect devastating, the foreplay occurring in smoky back rooms in small and big towns in Jersey, where the local politicos would benefit from giving special consideration to chemical, oil, and gas companies. When it first started, there wasn't the concern for the environment there was today, but it wouldn't have mattered anyway. Greed put blinders on when it came to such concerns.

Racanelli was on his way to Freehold, New Jersey, which was about seventy-five miles north of Atlantic City. Before too long, he thought, as he went further south, the gruesome scenery would pass and the turnpike would be flanked by regular countryside.

On another day, he knew, the scenery would not have bothered him as much. It was his destination that was coloring his perception.

His destination was the Golden View Nursing Home and Irmgard Werner's daughter, Rebecca, or Becky, as she called her.

Racanelli did not know much about Becky Werner. Basically he just knew her profession.

"Becky's a nurse," Irmgard had said, "in a private nursing home in Freehold. Takes care of old people. Very dedicated."

The night before, as he lay in bed, he realized that Becky would have to be informed of Irmgard's death.

He had thought briefly of contacting a clergyman or maybe just her superiors, but decided to do it himself. He owed Irmgard that, at least.

At around eight-thirty that morning he had called the Golden View and learned that Becky would be on duty until six in the evening.

He waited until the afternoon, when he had the results of the autopsy in hand. He wanted to be able to answer any medical questions she had. Looking at the details contained in the report, he hoped she didn't ask.

The two detectives assigned to guard him during the day were not thrilled when they learned he wanted to make the trip alone. But Racanelli reasoned that there was no way anyone was going to follow him. He would also be using a car that he had never used before.

The detectives were partially reassured by the fact that Racanelli was range-certified with a Baretta and he would take the gun with him.

He took a circuitous route out of the city, making a number of odd turns and maneuvers to make sure he wasn't being followed before crossing the George Washington Bridge and driving south until he got on the turnpike.

At one point the back-of-the-radio scenery gave way to flat, grassy countryside, now brownish green. Fifteen or twenty minutes later he got off at the exit for Freehold.

He found the nursing home without difficulty. The Golden View was located on a corner about six or seven blocks from what looked like the center of town. Like the rest of the homes in the area, it was big and old, with a large, sweeping, well-manicured lawn.

Racanelli parked on the street and went inside. There was a receptionist directly inside. He gave his name and was directed to wait in a small room off the foyer. He sat down on a couch and looked out the window, which faced the front of the house.

Becky Werner appeared in the doorway a minute after he sat down. She was wearing a sparkling white uniform and was thin, blonde, blue-eyed, pretty. It was easy to see she was Irmgard's daughter.

She was worried.

He stood up. He felt empty inside. There was no easy way to do this.

"Aren't you the district attorney?" she said.

Racanelli nodded.

"What's the matter?"

"I'm very sorry to say that your mother is dead."

"When? How?"

"Why don't you sit down?"

She went over to the couch and sat down. Racanelli sat down next to her. Her face was white. If he had wondered how she would react, he'd just found out.

"Would you like a drink of water or something?"

"No, thank you." She looked at Racanelli. "She start to drink again?"

"No. She was the victim of a homicide . . . in the course of a robbery at her apartment."

"Oh, my God," she said softly, "oh, my God."

Tears formed in her eyes. Racanelli touched her shoulder. She was quivering. He kept his hand there, then moved it toward her neck; he saw tears drop on her lap.

After a while, she got control of herself.

"How—how was she killed?"

"Knife."

Her eyes briefly searched Racanelli's face. For a moment he thought she was going to ask for details, but she didn't.

"How sad for her life to end like this," she said. "She was really coming back."

"No question."

"I really did think she'd make it. She—she spoke so highly of you. She loved the talks you had—that you were so important but still took the time to talk with her. It made her feel good."

"It was easy for me, she was a brave woman. Take it from me, there are very few people like your mother. I'm taking this personally."

Becky Werner nodded.

"I was hoping she might get married again," she said.

"I sensed there was someone in her life," Racanelli said.

"Yes. Someone named Ray Bloom. A doctor. I guess he should be notified."

"Do you have his number or address?"

"No, I really don't know all that much about him. My mother was secretive about him. Maybe you can find him. . . ."

"Sure, I'll find him. He live in Jersey?"

"No, New York."

"Do you know why she was secretive about him?"

"I don't know," she said, "but I know it made her happy. She dyed her hair, she was gaining weight, using lipstick. She . . ."

Becky Werner swallowed hard.

"I'll look into it," Racanelli said.

"Thank you."

"Where is Mom now?" Becky asked.

"Bellevue."

"I'd like to come in and take care of things."

"Can I drive you?"

"No, thank you. I have a friend . . . I'll go with him."

"Good. I'd like to know when the service is," Racanelli said. "You know the city will pay if—"

"I think I can afford it."

"I'd like to help," Racanelli said. "In any way I can. Let me give you my home number."

He wrote his number on one of his business cards and handed it to her.

"I don't know what to say."

Racanelli smiled.

"What's your number?"

She told him, and he wrote it down in a small notebook.

Racanelli stood. "I guess I'll be going."

"Thank you so much. I . . ."

Racanelli kissed her on the cheek.

"It's all right," he said.

CHAPTER 7

Frankenstein was sitting in their kitchen. It was ten in the morning, two days after they had made the Ferret in the Philadelphia morgue. There was a bottle of guinea red on the table between them.

Piccolo refilled his own glass. Stein was nursing his.

"It's just that I want you to understand the peril involved here, Howie. The peril in doing this to this fat fuck, and the peril with the brass."

Howie nodded. Piccolo slugged his wine.

"You see," he continued, "I don't know how—if this fat fuck finds us—how he would retaliate. These wops are big on respect. They don't like it when someone fucks them over, even a little. That's why I want to do it."

Stein nodded.

"And the brass," he said, "forget it. You and me are rounding the last bend. They find out about this and we better start looking for other work. I don't know about you, but I got enemies in the brass that would love to fuck me out of my pension."

"I think I do, too," Stein said. He paused, then spoke again.

"I understand the risk," Stein said, "but Capezzi must be hurt. The stars must be put into balance. If we don't do something, it will poison us. It's poisoning us now. We need to leech it from us now. In a way, we have no choice. Act—or die."

Piccolo continued, almost as if Stein hadn't spoken: "It's just that the Ferret was right about how shrewd Capezzi is.

The fucking DEA and half the Justice Department have been trying to figure out how to take him down for years and haven't been able to.

"Once," Piccolo went on, "the DEA tried to get a wire on him. They were totally unsuccessful. Capezzi has the shack he works out of, his house, and his car periodically swept for bugs. And I don't know what else he does. Who his friends are. This is a guy with millions of bucks. You can buy a lot of people in high places.

Piccolo took another drink of wine.

"I thought about whacking Capezzi," he said, "but no, that's not right. For my partner, yeah. But not the Ferret. And if you keep doing that, you're not a cop anymore, just a killer."

"You have to draw a line. That could poison you, too."

"And you know, no matter what we do, it's probably never going to make us feel completely better."

"I know that, too."

"But you remember the picture *The Sting*, with Paul what's-his-name?"

"Newman."

"Yeah. At the end of that picture he tells the other guy—Redford—that what they did to the bad guy could never equal what the bad guy had done to them . . . and Redford agrees. But then Newman says: 'But it was close, wasn't it?' And Redford smiles and says: 'Yeah, yeah. It was close.' "

Stein smiled. Piccolo summed up their plans:

"This is our option now, the best we can do. Just squeeze his stones until his eyes pop out of his motherfucking dago gangster wop head."

They raised their glasses in a toast.

"*Mazel Tov!*" Stein said.

And they clinked glasses.

CHAPTER 8

On Sunday morning, five days after they agreed to put the squeeze on Capezzi's stones, Frankenstein was in Piccolo's Trans Am, tooling east on the Long Island Expressway. It was only nine o'clock and traffic was fairly light, by no means the usual case on the famed six-lane road that ran east and west across Long Island.

As planned, they were on their own time, not due back on the job until four in the afternoon of the next day. Plenty of time to do what they wanted to do.

They both felt good. Very good. Almost festive.

"Sal," Piccolo had said earlier in the week when they first had the idea, "owes me a favor. He would of done a big bit if it wasn't for me. I had the DA reduce a heavy burglary to a misdemeanor."

Piccolo had been talking about Sal D'Amico, who they were now on their way to see.

"He comes," Piccolo had explained, "from a good family. His father was on the job, but after he and the old lady got unhitched, the kids went fucking wild. Ray," he said, referring to Sal's father, "he was no saint, either. Drank his ass off. Got fucked up. So the kids got fucked up, too. I did it for Ray . . . He died a couple of years ago."

"Does Sal know what we're going to do?" Stein asked.

Piccolo looked at him and smiled wolfishly.

"The less he fucking knows," he said, "the better for his health."

* * *

Sal D'Amico lived in Greenlawn, a part of Huntington, Long Island, that was considered the wrong side of the tracks. Most of the area, which was about a mile square, contained small private homes, many of which were rentals and had a kind of rundown look compared to the rest of the town, where homes and lawns were well maintained. In the suburbs nothing was as important to most homeowners as their property.

D'Amico lived in a small house adjacent to a large packed-dirt area that served as his driveway. In it were parked a truck and a shiny customized black Blazer with the legend NIGHT LIGHT written across the bumper in red script. There were also a couple of dilapidated cars that had been half restored by Sal and his brother Lou, who lived in the house with their old ladies.

Frankenstein got to D'Amico's house at about ten o'clock and parked on the street.

Piccolo, a car freak himself, immediately went up to the Blazer. He was admiring it when Sal came out of a side entrance to the house. He was a tall skinny kid with longish black hair. He wore scuffed boots, chinos, and a black body shirt. His skinny arms were heavily tattooed.

"Mr. Piccolo, how are you?"

"Good, Sal," Piccolo said, shaking his hand when he came up to him. "Staying out of trouble?"

"Definitely."

"Good man," Piccolo said, and turned toward Stein, who had come up beside him. "This is my partner, Sal. Howie Stein."

Sal shook Stein's hand.

"Nice rig here," Piccolo said. "You got a lot of bucks in it?"

"Yeah. But all honest, Mr. Piccolo."

"I have no doubt," Piccolo said, smiling.

"Can I take a look at yours?"

"Always happy to show off my baby."

The three men went over to the Trans Am. Piccolo and D'Amico talked animatedly about it for a minute or so. Stein stood nearby, about as interested as he would have been in attending a seminar on bus design.

After a couple of minutes more, Piccolo said:

"I want to thank you for the use of the truck."

"You're welcome," D'Amico said. "Would you like me to show you how the honeywagon works?"

"Please," Piccolo said.

Frankenstein became very attentive.

The truck, an eighteen-wheeler, had a red Peterbilt cab and, behind it, a silver-painted cylindrical tank. On the side was the legend, printed in black: S & S SANITATION. On the front and rear bumpers was written in red script: WE'RE NUMBER 1 IN THE NUMBER 2 BUSINESS.

D'Amico showed Frankenstein everything. It took about a half hour, and they punctuated his very clear explanation with questions.

"And it's loaded, like you wanted," D'Amico said when he was finished. "Full to the brim—three thousand gallons."

"Great," Piccolo said.

To be on the safe side, they took the truck for a run, Piccolo driving under the watchful eye of Sal for fifteen minutes. Then Sal watched as Howie worked the cylinder apparatus.

Finally Frankenstein was finished.

"We'll have it back before you go to work tomorrow," Piccolo said. "If we're delayed, I'll call."

"No problem," Sal said, "whatever."

Piccolo backed the truck out of the driveway. On the street they waved to D'Amico, and then were gone down the block.

CHAPTER 9

Frankenstein started for Philadelphia at around nine at night; that would get them there in the wee hours of the morning.

Both men were dressed in green work clothes that they had bought a couple of days earlier in a secondhand store off Fordham Road. Three days ago they had made a dry run to Philly by car, so they knew exactly what they were going to do during the wet run, assuming no unforeseen things.

They had to make one stop before hitting Philly, and had found it in the town of Masefield Square, which was less than a half hour from the city.

They both carried their shields, their service revolvers, and a 30-30, in case things got sticky. They figured that wasn't likely, since they were making the run in the middle of the night.

"Who the fuck's going to be there?" Piccolo wondered.

Still, they knew that the operation was going to take some time. Somebody might show up.

They didn't want to carry offbeat firepower in case they were stopped by a cop. This way they could just claim they were undercovers.

They got off at the Masefield Square exit, making a long, sweeping turn up the exit road. They glanced both ways, then Piccolo swung the big truck to the right, proceeding down Route 24, which was flanked by large, modernistic office buildings.

They had picked the fourth one down on the right; a big,

squat, squarish building that seemed to be made completely of glass.

There were no lights behind any of the windows, just short post lights flanking a broad concrete path that led to the front doors and a light over the front doors. Frankenstein also knew that there was a light over a rear entrance.

They had seen one car when they got on Route 24, and no traffic as Piccolo turned the big truck onto the driveway on the side that led to the rear parking area.

The parking area was empty, except for a few scattered cars—just like it had been when they had made their dry run.

Piccolo turned the truck off and he and Stein were out of it quickly, each bearing a huge roll of duct tape.

Piccolo worked one side of the truck, Stein the other. Each man worked the same way. Sticking the end of the tape at one end of the S & S logo, then drawing the tape down and adhering it firmly.

Within ten minutes both logos had been covered.

Then they covered the two slogans on the bumpers.

"I would have liked to have left it," Piccolo said, as they pulled out of the parking lot. Five minutes later they were on the turnpike.

When they'd left New York, Frankenstein had mainly told what cops called "war stories," escapades and exploits they'd been involved in on the job.

Or they had groused about the "young shits," as Piccolo said, that were flowing out the academy and what this would mean for the N.Y.P.D. as the years went by.

"Shit in, shit out. Right, Howie?" Piccolo had said at one point.

"I'm afraid you're right," Howie had said.

They also talked about women. Piccolo said that all Stein had to do was give the word and he would set him up with a broad as soon as they got back. Piccolo himself went out with a different broad every week.

But Howie demurred. His wife, Betty, was now somewhere in California with their two children, Jennifer and Howie, Jr. Stein had taken a real bad burn from her. One day he had returned to their picturesque little home in Massapequa, Long Island, to find nothing there except hangers in the closets. He was understandably reluctant to get involved with a woman, and he couldn't take the route Frank took.

The volume of talk had been fairly constant, but from the moment they got on the turnpike the volume decreased. They were like two soldiers going into battle, each with the same thought: To stick it far up into Capezzi and then break it off.

Or, as Howie had put it:

"The stars have to be put back in their proper order," and Piccolo had affirmed it with a more direct: "Fuckin' A right."

They took the Walt Whitman Bridge across the Delaware River into Pennsylvania, past Veterans Stadium, and then, briefly, across the fringes of Philly, made a left at Penrose Street, then tooled down Penrose, crossing the Schuylkill River, the Ferret's last resting place.

Capezzi, they had learned, had moved his auto junkyard operation from Delaware to Penrose. Penrose was a nice-sounding name, but it hardly described the street itself, a pastiche of junkyards and refineries, Philadelphia's industrial section, with the nickname the "asshole of the city."

The street was empty.

"Let's go by it one time," Piccolo said.

Stein nodded.

They proceeded up the block at a normal speed.

They passed Tiny's Used Auto Parts, formerly Union Auto Parts and the place Tiny Capezzi operated out of.

It was a long, white mobile home set on blocks. There

were three or four small windows in front and on the side. Behind the home was the junkyard, surrounded by a high Cyclone fence topped with vicious concertina wire.

Frankenstein also knew there were pit bull terriers in the yard. During the dry run Piccolo had walked to the fence and two of them had leaped up on the fence, trying to get at him.

They went past Tiny's. Piccolo hung the first right he could, then another right onto Penrose again.

Frankenstein glanced at each other but said nothing. It was going to be a wet run.

Piccolo pulled up in front of the shack, motor running. Stein clambered down out of the cab. He had a big brace and spade bit in his right hand. He went over to a window to the right of the door, then to the other two.

He went back to the cab and said:

"I think there's a dog in there."

"Fuck him," Piccolo said. "You live like a dog, you die like a dog!" And he cackled.

Then Stein went over to the door, stood in front, and jumped up, grabbing the top edge of the shack with his thunderfist arm. He pulled himself onto the roof. From inside there was a single guttural bark, but the dog really started to bark when Stein started to drill into the roof.

Piccolo, meanwhile, had pulled the truck up a bit and, leaving the motor running, was out of the cab and over to the side of the truck closest to the shack.

He unhooked the hose, pulled out twenty feet of it, then ran the end over to where Stein was working on the roof.

Piccolo waited until Stein appeared, then fed the hose, which was fairly stiff, up until Stein could grab it.

Stein fed the end of the hose five or six feet across the roof and then a good two feet through the hole he had drilled.

The dog was going bananas, barking and leaping up at the hose.

"Turn it on."

Piccolo turned it on. A pump kicked off and the contents of the truck started to flow into the shack.

Within seconds, the smell of rotten eggs filled the air. The dog continued to bark.

And who wouldn't, Piccolo thought, if the place he was in was filling up with shit?

Then, spontaneously, both men started to cackle and howl, their arms stretched to the sky, a smell around them only cops with autopsy-proof stomachs could handle without puking, the stench so thick and oppressive you could cut it with a knife.

How sweet it was!

Frankenstein waited until they were out of Philadelphia proper, on the turnpike heading north, before making the calls.

They made three. One was to the *Philadelphia Enquirer*, two were to two local TV stations.

"Hey," he said to all, "check out Tiny's Auto Parts on 2134 Penrose. Somebody just dumped about fourteen tons of shit into the shack. You know, the headquarters of Angelo Capezzi, the Mafia hump. But bring boots and a gas mask!"

Chapter 10

The house was set on a woodsy, sloping acre of land close to the downtown area of Philadelphia. It was a large, white stucco, one-story house with a red-tile roof. The property was rimmed by a high, spiked, wrought-iron fence. It was a most unusual-looking house for the area, which mostly had standard wood-frame construction with siding and shingled roofs.

The owner of the home, Angelo "Tiny" Capezzi, who was sitting in a large, ornate, Mediterranean-style armchair, was unusual-looking, too.

He weighed, as someone once said, "as much as a car, but a car was better-looking."

Indeed. He had thick lips, goiterish eyes, and a flat, froglike nose, pockmarked skin, and was bald except for fringes of gray hair on the sides of his head. Someone once said that he resembled Jabba the Hutt, the character in the movie *Star Wars 2*.

Capezzi was watching the news and doing what he did almost all the time: eating. Now he was working on his second pepperoni pizza, which was on a small table next to the chair, within reach of a pudgy hand. He ate slowly but steadily, occasionally sipping diet Pepsi from a two-liter bottle, also on the table.

Sitting in an adjacent armchair, also watching the TV, was Aldo Antonio, one of Capezzi's many button men, a huge man in his midthirties who was built more like Arnold Schwarzenegger than Jabba the Hutt. Like all of Capezzi's goons, he wore the unofficial official uniform: a dark suit, white shirt, and dark tie. He also looked like he had been in the ring awhile, which was true. He had had seventeen fights as a heavyweight, fifteen of them fixed.

Aldo seemed calm outside, but he was anxious inside. He just knew that Capezzi was angry, and it made him edgy.

It was five-ten in the evening of the same day that Frankenstein had visited Capezzi's shack.

The announcer was a middle-aged man named Bud Keen, and the close observer—and Angelo Capezzi was a close observer—would notice that Keen had a twinkle in his eye even though he was reporting the incident using language that was dry, delicate, and devoid of double entendres.

Keen told of "vandals who pumped thousands of gallons of raw sewage into the mobile home–style headquarters of reputed mobster Angelo "Tiny" Capezzi on Penrose," and then "alerted" the media to what they had done.

He went on to say that police emergency service workers had to don protective gear and breathing apparatus before opening the door and that, unfortunately, a pit bull terrier "drowned on the premises."

Interspersed in Keen's report was film footage of the shack—showing how the sewage had seeped out from doors and windows.

They also had an interview with a housing authority official who said that the building would have to be "condemned."

Keen added that the police were investigating, but had "no leads."

Keen then went on to another topic, but just before he did, his lips formed the slightest smile and his face got a tiny bit redder.

He managed to hold back the laugh.

Capezzi continued to eat. There was no expression on his face, he was thinking about who might have done it.

There were times when he would get into territorial disputes with other families, but as far as he could see there was no problem with that now. So it probably wasn't one of them.

Then he started to think of this guy or that who had something against him. There were hundreds of people who would want to hurt him.

He gave that up. There were just too many.

How about someone close to him? Like Aldo, or maybe Tony? Were they working with someone else to fuck him up?

He didn't think so.

His brother Guido?

No.

Finally he spoke:

"Find out who did this, Aldo."

"Yes, sir," Aldo said.

CHAPTER 11

On a Friday morning, about a week after he had gone to see Becky Werner, Racanelli was sitting at his desk, having some difficulty concentrating. Irmgard Werner was now dead and buried and there had been little progress on the case.

The only positive thing, if you could call it that, was that Onairuts had found a single blond hair entwined in Irmgard's pubic hair. It did not belong to Irmgard.

Onairuts said there was no indication that she had been sexually assaulted, and they did not find any semen in her body cavities.

He stood up and went over to the large window that overlooked the Grand Concourse.

He had a good view of Joyce Kilmer Park, a broad, flat park filled with rolling greens, ball courts, and a track.

Here and there he could see clusters of people, some people playing handball, and a lone runner on the track . . . .

Where, he thought, was Dr. Bloom? They had put all the usual lines in the water and had come up with nothing.

What kind of boyfriend could he be? He hadn't been around in a week. Or, if he had, he hadn't let on.

Maybe that was it. He couldn't let on. Maybe he was cheating on his wife or something—

The intercom buzzed. Racanelli went back to the desk and picked up.

It was his secretary, Marge Bachman.

"Joe Lawless on thirty-two," she said.

Racanelli picked up.

"Hey, Joe, how's it going?"

"Better," he said.

"What have you got?"

"We located an old black guy who said he saw Irmgard with a guy two days before she got killed."

"Where?"

"Coming out of the DeLuxe Theatre on Fordham Road."

"Make the guy?"

"No. Just described him. In his forties. Blond hair."

"Really?"

"Yeah. Totally blond, thinning a bit."

"Good," Racanelli said.

"There's more," Lawless said. "This same guy thinks he remembers them getting into a red car. I showed him pictures. . . . He picked out a red Corvette."

"Excellent."

"We're going to work the DeLuxe and the area around it to see what we can see."

There was a pause.

"Nothing from the boyfriend yet?" Lawless asked.

"No."

"If this guy exists, no one has seen him out here."

"It's odd," Racanelli said.

"Very."

"Keep in touch, Joe."

"You got it."

Chapter 12

The next morning, at about ten-thirty, Joe Lawless entered the Department of Social Services building on Southern Boulevard in the Bronx. The building was a battered brick job with barred windows.

Lawless had an appointment to see a man named Vincent Spano, Irmgard Werner's caseworker.

Lawless identified himself to a heavy black woman sitting at a battered desk in the hall; she turned her head and called Spano's name. He appeared at the door that led to interior offices a minute later.

He was short, dark haired, wore glasses. His eyes darted about as he offered a damp hand. It was not, Lawless thought, the easiest job in the world.

Lawless followed Spano into a large, high-ceilinged room filled with lines of desks.

Spano led Lawless to his own desk, which was near the middle of the room. At his invitation, Lawless sat down.

"This is her file," Spano said, touching a large brown folder on the desk. "I don't know exactly what you need, but I'll help you as much as I can."

"Thanks," Lawless said, "I just need to know a few things. First, how long was Ms. Werner a client of yours?"

"A year and a half. Two years this March."

"What was the routine? Did she come here? Or did you go to see her?"

"Well, she would come here. But not that often. She was only required to come in every six months to be recertified—declared eligible for assistance. I saw her last"—he glanced at the file—"last August. August sixth."

"That was the last time you spoke to her?"

Spano leafed through the file with fingers that had nails bitten to the quick.

"No. I spoke with her on the phone six, seven weeks ago. September fifth."

"What about?"

Spano furrowed his brow, then he responded.

"It's hard to remember, but I think it was just to see how she was doing."

Lawless nodded.

"Had things changed or something since you saw her in August?"

Spano took a moment to answer.

"No, sometimes people call us—or we call them—just to keep in touch, head off any problems that might be developing."

"I see," Lawless said. "Did she at any time mention having a boyfriend? Or were you aware of her having one?"

Spano's face screwed up in a mass of fine wrinkles.

"No, I wasn't."

"Did you get any sense that she was worried about anything?"

"She seemed in good spirits, I would say."

Lawless nodded.

"Do you know who her friends are?"

Spano shook his head, but then said:

"She has a daughter in New Jersey. Freehold. But I don't

know any of her friends. Do you want her daughter's address?"

Lawless shook his head.

"All right, Mr. Spano," Lawless said, standing up. "I think that's about it. Thanks for your help."

"No problem."

Spano smiled.

"Anything else, just call."

Lawless shook his hand. It seemed even more damp than when he had first come in.

Spano walked Lawless to the door, then went back to his desk. He waited about ten or fifteen seconds, then reached for the phone and tapped out a number.

He watched the closed door as the phone rang.

Chapter 13

After speaking with Spano, Lawless intended to canvass the Fordham area where Werner had been spotted with the blond-haired guy. But he had a problem: he had no current pictures of her.

He solved the problem in a rather ghoulish way and hoped that prospective witnesses wouldn't notice. He had a blowup made of a morgue shot. Unless you knew, it looked like Werner was sleeping.

Whatever, the photo was as good as he was going to get. He had a half-dozen copies of it made.

Lawless also got duplicate photos made of the red Corvette that he had shown the witness. He couldn't be sure he would be showing the right model, but one thing about a Corvette: the styling had stayed basically the same over the years.

He also knew that some people could recognize cars as easily as faces.

As busy as the Felony Squad was, Lawless got two of his detectives—Byron and Clinton—to help him canvass. He told them it might be best to present Irmgard, the car, and the blond-haired guy as a package, as well as individually. Sometimes people would remember parts of scenes, sometimes an entire scene.

They started canvassing the area in the evening.

First stop for Lawless was the DeLuxe Theatre. Lawless showed the pictures to the same ticket seller who'd been on duty the day the old man said he'd spotted Irmgard and the guy coming out of the theater.

The ticket seller, a middle-aged black woman, looked at the pictures a long time but said that she didn't recognize anyone—or the car.

While he was questioning the ticket seller, Byron and Clifton started to show the pictures up and down the block. As soon as Lawless had finished with the ticket seller, he joined them.

The detectives took two hours and covered a three-block radius of the theater—bodegas, laundromats, a supermarket, check-cashing places, another ticket seller in an adjacent theater, restaurants, discount stores.

Nothing.

He expanded the canvass a bit to cover some of the apartment buildings in the area.

But it was slow going here. Many of the people were leery about opening doors, and many regarded The Man as an enemy. Cooperation was not free-flowing.

They did get one possible hit, though.

A young Spanish guy told Clinton he had seen a red Corvette on the street, but no people around it, and he didn't remember the plate number. He said it was parked on the north side of Valentine Avenue, one of the number of blocks that fed into Fordham Road. It was just around the corner from the DeLuxe.

Lawless wasn't sure if the kid was telling the truth. He had a macho, know-it-all kind of way about him, was the kind of guy, Lawless sensed, who couldn't admit he didn't know something.

Lawless disbanded the search at about eleven-thirty.

He made a note to himself to check out the multilevel garage on Fordham and Jerome. Even though it was a good walk from the DeLuxe, maybe the guy had parked there. Not many people would be comfortable leaving a red Corvette on the streets of Fort Siberia.

Instead of going home himself, Lawless went to the squad room.

There were a number of other detectives there, but it didn't bother him. Over his years as a detective, he'd learned to think in a crowd—and thinking was what he wanted to do now.

He poured himself a cup of coffee, sat down at one of the gray iron desks, and put his feet up. He stared across the large, bile-green room.

He thought about the knife wounds. She had been stabbed four times—and, of course, her throat had been cut.

The throat wound had severed the hyoid bone and two of the knife thrusts had pierced her pericardium. Someone wanted her dead.

But who was it? Lover—or thief? Or was it someone else altogether?

He sat back down at the desk. He resisted the urge for a cigarette.

He thought about the defensive wounds. Standard. Told him nothing.

There was nothing under her nails, no blood on her except her own.

He tried to imagine the way she was done.

Onairuts, he thought, had confirmed that she had been done in the wee hours.

Okay. She's in bed. The window was open. And he came in.

She sees him, and he is on her—that's why there was so much blood on the bed.

They fight, she's fighting for her life, you get arterial spray everywhere.

She is up, on her feet, struggling next to the bed. Then she exsanguinates, loses consciousness, goes down. She probably landed face down—Onairuts did say that her face was bruised—so the killer didn't stab her again. He knew she was finished.

Lawless felt the urge for a cigarette again. He thought about how his wife, Barbara, who was also a cop at the Five Three, was on his back to stop. He smiled, remembered something she had said.

"You know, if we have a final confrontation on this, remember that we're both armed!"

Lawless's mind flicked back to the case, to the pubic hair, that single blond strand.

Unfortunately the hair did not have a root. If it did, they could have done DNA testing on it.

But what they had was better than nothing.

He finished the last of the coffee and stood up.

Lawless realized he wasn't even close to having any answers. He would simply have to keep digging.

CHAPTER 14

After returning the honeywagon to Sal D'Amico in Greenlawn, and following their four-to-twelve tour, Frankenstein debated whether or not to go down to Philly to get another look at Capezzi's shack.

It would have been sweet, but maybe too dangerous. Capezzi would certainly have his hoods sniffing around as to who might have done the deed.

They decided against going.

But they knew they couldn't settle for doing nothing, so the next day they traveled down to Times Square, to newsstands where out-of-town papers were sold. They bought the *Philadelphia Daily News* and the *Philadelphia Enquirer*, two big papers.

Both papers carried the story—one on page two and one on page three—and the reporters and headline writers made merry. Frankenstein particularly liked the one in the *News:*

TINY'S FULL HOUSE NEEDS A ROYAL FLUSH

The story recounted what had happened, then had a Philly PD captain's comment that the action was a misdemeanor and that the police could only spend a limited amount of time "trying to get a lead on the perpetrators."

"Ain't that a shame," Piccolo said.

"Yeah," Stein said, "a really cosmic tragedy."

Frankenstein particularly liked what the reporter in the *Enquirer* wrote. He said that when a man at the scene who seemed to work for Capezzi was asked for a comment, he had replied with a "gruff expletive."

"Yeah," Piccolo cackled, "like get out of here, motherfucker!"

All of the papers said that Angelo Capezzi had not responded to telephone inquiries.

"Yeah," Piccolo said, making Howie really titter, "he was too busy breaking up the fucking furniture."

Frankenstein had taken the subway to get to Manhattan from the Bronx, and they also took it back. They were looking for action, hoping to get accosted, assaulted, to play bunker fish—potential victims—in a game cops called "trolling for bluefish."

To make it more likely, they sat on opposite sides of the car, giving no indication whatsoever that they knew each other.

Ideally Frankenstein hoped they would run into one of those wolf packs that periodically roamed the trains, streets, and parks of the city, terrorizing citizens. Say a group with the size and soul of the pack that nearly killed the jogger in Central Park. That would be great.

Both men also traveled the subways when they were alone, but that was not a good idea. Having backup was much smarter.

On two previous occasions there had been trouble—both times involving Piccolo.

One time he had come to the assistance of a young patrolman who was pursuing a perp who had snatched some gold. That was nothing much.

The other had involved two brothers approaching him on a train late at night. He was on his way uptown after seeing the Knicks game at the Garden.

They had approached him and unsubtly asked for all his money.

The question had elicited a response that set off an alarm

bell in the belly of one of the perps. A response, the perp had decided, which was unnatural: the man's face was afraid, but his *eyes* were not. They seemed happy. Motherfucking weird.

That perp, whose name was Bubba, wanted to abort the thing, but he decided to see it through. He didn't want to seem pussy to his partner, whose name was Steve.

Within thirty seconds, Piccolo had the situation under control; he had one inch of his .38 up the left nostril of Bubba, who had promptly lost control of his bladder.

Piccolo then asked them to make a move on him so he would have an excuse to shoot them both.

"I haven't shot anyone in a week," he said. "How about it?"

But they didn't accommodate him.

Now, as they traveled uptown, the train rattled along through the tunnel, both men were only half concentrating on their roles as victims. They had decided to think of something else: another way to squeeze Tiny Capezzi's balls.

The dump job was not enough. It only partly filled them. They needed to do more. They needed to hurt Capezzi until his fat ass puckered.

Soon the train ride was over and they were walking along Fordham toward the precinct. No one had even scoped them.

"Come up with anything?" Piccolo said.

"I have a couple of ideas," Stein said, "but I want to develop them more fully."

"I got some ideas, too," Piccolo said. "but I don't want to do just any old thing."

Chapter 15

For Racanelli, this Sunday was different. Though he was spending it at home, as he usually did, he was not working.

He didn't feel like it, and he knew why. In his own way, he was in mourning for Irmgard. Out of the blue he would think about her and would feel a little pang of sadness that she was gone.

Racanelli knew he wouldn't get morbid about it. He had the ability to bounce back quickly—a necessity in his job.

It was around eleven o'clock. He and his mother had gone to the ten o'clock mass, then, as usual, stopped at Lara's Bakery for rolls and goodies, most of which Mama would end up giving away.

He also bought about thirty pounds of newspapers, and on the way home stopped to talk to four or five hundred people.

By eleven-thirty, he had changed from the suit he wore to church into casual clothes. He was sitting on the old-fashioned couch in the living room reading the *Times*.

The rituals were in full swing. The air was redolent with the rich tang of spaghetti sauce, which his mother was preparing in the kitchen. From the stereo came the heroic sounds of Caruso that Pop had loved so much.

Around noon, she called him in to taste the sauce, just as Pop had done for years. It was, of course, delicious.

"*Buena*, Mama," he said, "*perfectamente*," speaking to her, as he often did, in her native Italian.

She smiled her usual smile, and Racanelli returned to the living room to read.

Such days were so great for him.

There was only one thing missing: Pop.

Sometimes, though, he would sense that his father was still alive, in the house. That Racanelli could go into the kitchen, the way he used to, and his father would be there, sitting at the kitchen table, sipping a glass of Cappuccino, and he would say something like:

"Onofrio"—Pop never used his nickname—"how's abouta you and me—we walk and talk."

He used to love those walks with his father. He loved holding his incredibly big, rough hand—he was a brick layer—and walking around the neighborhood. Without fail, his father would stop to talk with all his old cronies congregating in front of their houses, and then they might walk to Fordham University and watch people play ball, or just look at the beautiful old brick buildings that Pop loved.

And they would talk. To young Ono, they were just meaningless conversations, but then, as he grew up, he came to realize that in Pop's mind he was getting his son ready for life, teaching him everything he knew. . . .

Around twelve-thirty, Racanelli felt himself getting a little sleepy. He was just drifting off when he heard the phone start to ring. His mother picked up in the kitchen, then appeared in the hall doorway.

"For you, Ono," she said in Italian. "Joe Lawless."

Racanelli picked up in the hall. "Joe, how's it going?"

"Fine. I just got back a bunch of mud sheets," he said, referring to records that detailed local calls, "and I think we should get together and talk."

"Have you eaten?"

"No."

"Want a spaghetti dinner? My mother's making a couple of tons of it."

''Oh. I was planning on having coffee and a cigarette . . . but you've twisted my arm. I'm on my way.''

Racanelli chuckled, then hung up. He realized he was excited. What did Lawless have?

Chapter 16

Racanelli used the walkie-talkie to alert the team of cops sitting in the sedan across the street from his house that Joe Lawless was coming.

Ryan, one of the cops, said:

''We know him, sir. No problem.''

Fifteen minutes later, Lawless showed up.

Racanelli brought him into the kitchen to say hello to his mother, who greeted him warmly. Lawless, who had blond hair and resembled the late actor Steve McQueen, had long ago realized that he was treated in a special way by Italian women—indeed, his wife Barbara was Italian.

He and Racanelli went into the living room. Lawless pulled a thin sheaf of papers from his jacket pocket.

''Let's go over here,'' Racanelli said.

They both sat down on the couch. Lawless spread the papers across the table.

''These are the September and October mud sheets from the public phone in the Miramar lobby. I thought they might give us a lead on Bloom. But notice the numbers I've marked in red.''

Mud sheets were appropriately nicknamed. The printing, done on thin, glossy paper was small and blurred, just readable.

Each entry carried the number called, the time, the number called from, and the date.

Racanelli looked.

Six entries had been underlined. Three calls in September, three in October.

"Same number. Who's is it?"

"Spano's direct number," Lawless said. "I got it the first time I called him."

Racanelli's brow furrowed.

"Spano said the last time he spoke with Irmgard was . . . ?"

"September sixth."

"He lied. Why?"

"I don't know," Lawless said.

"How do you want to handle it?" Racanelli asked.

"Let's just show up, whack him. No appointment."

"Good," Racanelli said. "I want to be with you."

"Fine."

"Tomorrow morning?"

"Sounds good to me."

"What about Bloom?"

"So far, nothing."

A short while later, Racanelli's mother called them in to eat. The meal was delicious, but not as tasty as what was on tomorrow morning's menu.

CHAPTER 17

On Monday morning at eight-fifteen Lawless met Racanelli in front of the Social Services building on Southern Boulevard. They went in immediately.

On the second floor, Lawless went up to the receptionist, the same one who'd been on the desk before, showed his shield, and said:

"Mr. Spano in?"

"Yes."

"He's expecting me," Lawless said, "I'll just go in."

"Okay."

Lawless went in, followed by Racanelli.

Lawless spotted Spano at his desk. Some of the other caseworkers had clients at their desks, but Spano was alone, his head down. He did not see Lawless.

Lawless and Racanelli headed toward him.

Spano looked up when they were a few feet from him. A look of surprise—maybe fear—played across his face. He remained seated.

"Mr. Lawless. What are you doing here?"

"We have to talk," Lawless said. He was grim.

"About what?"

"It's private. You got a place?"

Spano's face had lost some color.

"We can use one of the empty offices," he said. His voice was reedy.

He led them across the room; the supervisors' office—real rooms with real doors—were banked along one long wall. Spano walked toward one whose door was closed.

He opened the door slowly: The office was empty.

"We can use this." His voice was still shaky.

The empty office contained a desk, a couple of chairs, filing cabinets. No one could accuse welfare supervisors of being on the take.

Lawless closed the door behind them. Spano had taken up a position at the front of the desk. Lawless joined Racanelli, who was standing opposite Spano.

"I'd like you to meet Onofrio Racanelli, district attorney of Bronx County," Lawless said.

Spano started to stick out his hand, but when Racanelli made no attempt to shake it he pulled it back.

"Mr. Spano, why did you lie about speaking to Irmgard Werner?" Racanelli asked. Racanelli's unblinking dark eyes were fixed on Spano.

"What?"

"Isn't the question clear? Let me put it another way. When was the last time you spoke with Irmgard Werner?"

"I told you," Spano said, his eyes flitting to Lawless.

"You said September sixth," Lawless said.

"Yes."

"That's a lie, Mr. Spano. You spoke with her on September sixth, seventeenth, twenty-third, October fourth, seventh, and fifteenth—two days before her death," Racanelli said, speaking low and fast.

Spano looked at the worn plain gray tile floor.

"There—there are a lot of people I speak to. I can't remember everyone."

Racanelli spoke. His voice was hard and cold.

"You have records. You noted September sixth, why not the other dates?"

It was obvious that Spano was feeling like a butterfly pinned to a board.

"How could you forget speaking with someone who was murdered after your last conversation with her?"

Spano said nothing.

They were a couple of yards apart. Racanelli stepped toward him.

"Look, Mr. Spano," he said, his voice metallic, "Irmgard Werner was a friend of mine. This is personal, so don't lie to me. I'll give you one more chance. Why did you lie about not speaking with her?"

Spano blinked. Lawless and Racanelli could see the gears turning inside his head.

"I have nothing further to say," he said. "If you want to talk with me, I'll give you the name of my attorney."

He hesitated a minute, then opened the door, and left the room.

Racanelli and Lawless watched him go.

"Open this up, Joe," Racanelli said. "Find out what this bastard is hiding."

"You got it," Lawless said.

Chapter 18

Twenty-four hours after they started thinking about it, Frankenstein figured they had a good general idea, but to find out if it was workable, they needed to know some details about Capezzi.

To get them, Stein called a guy he knew at the ATF. To cover his tracks as much as possible, Stein asked his friend there, a guy named Johnson, for the same information on three wise guys so as not to highlight Capezzi.

The ATF had terrific data, a computer network that was tied into all kinds of information about anyone in the country, a mountain of facts from IRS, the services, public documents, and on and on and on.

A half hour after Stein made the request, Johnson was back on the line telling him everything he wanted to know.

On Friday, just five days after the dump job on the shack, Frankenstein left for Philadelphia after an eight-to-four. This time they went down in Piccolo's Trans Am and with only a single piece of equipment. Just to be on the safe side, they hung some plates from an impounded car.

The beauty of the idea, they agreed, was its simplicity.

They waited until they got into Philadelphia before making the call. It was, they thought, the prudent thing to do. They didn't want to give Capezzi enough time to figure out what was going down.

Piccolo's philosophy here was the same as in a fight: "Talk to him after you tear his head off."

They made the call from outside a diner on Passyunk Avenue, tapping out the home number Johnson had given Stein.

Piccolo did the calling after winning a coin flip for the right an hour earlier.

When the phone started to ring, Piccolo held the phone so Howie, who was standing next to him, could hear.

The phone rang twice.

"Yeah?" The voice was what you would expect. Deep and sandpapery.

"Is Mr. Capezzi there?"

"Who's this?"

"This is the guys who filled his trailer up with shit."

Silence.

Piccolo and Stein were beaming.

"Who the fuck is this?"

"Hey," Piccolo said, "some of that shit get in your ears? Put that fat fuck on!"

Sandpaper voice hung up. Piccolo tapped the number out again.

It rang once and was picked up. But the person who answered did not speak. Piccolo did.

"Don't hang up, hump," he said, "because if you do, Mr. Capezzi may hold you responsible for what's going to happen. He may spank you, motherfucker."

The phone was put down. Then Piccolo heard talking in the distance. Then he heard someone approach the phone.

"Yeah?"

Piccolo just knew it was Jabba the Hutt himself.

"Capezzi," Piccolo said, "like I was explaining to the moron who answered the phone, we're the guys who filled up your shack with shit."

"Do you know who I am?"

"Sure, that's why it's so much fun," Piccolo said, making Howie titter.

There was no response from Capezzi, but Piccolo thought he could feel heat coming through the wire.

Piccolo spoke.

"We heard," he said, "that you got a new fucking shack. After all, if you took away the old one, and didn't put in a new one, we wouldn't have no new place to put our new load of shit."

Piccolo followed this with a high, cackling laugh and was joined by Howie's titter. It sounded like they were playing a tape from a psycho ward.

The laughter died down after twenty seconds. Capezzi had stayed on the line.

"You a smart guy," Capezzi said, "you forget this stuff."

"Shut up you swinish motherfucker, and listen," Piccolo said. "We're calling to tell you that we're going to do more bad shit to your property. All kinds of bad shit. When we're finished, you'll long for the days of the shack."

Howie tittered. Once Frank got going he killed him.

''What do you want?'' Capezzi said, his voice low but strained. ''Why you breaking my stones?''

''Because we enjoy it,'' Stein said, ''very much. Embarrassing you, making you look like a fool, hurting you, ruining your property. That's why.''

''Couldn't of said it better myself,'' Piccolo said.

And then commenced more cackle-titter tape from the psycho ward.

Capezzi hung up.

''I think he's annoyed,'' Piccolo said.

''I think you're right,'' Howie said.

Chapter 19

As soon as he hung up, Capezzi went to the refrigerator and put three pounds of red grapes in a bowl. Then he sat down at the kitchen table, started to inhale them, and called Aldo in.

Capezzi detailed to Aldo what the guys on the phone said, and that Capezzi thought that they probably weren't playing with ''a full deck.''

''I'll get some people watching the shack,'' Aldo said, ''right away.''

''Also beef up people at the house here.''

''Yes, sir.''

''That's it?''

Capezzi thought: he had a boat, a Jag that was in the shop, and various pieces of real estate that he didn't think these humps knew about. In fact, they probably didn't know about anything. The trailer was a fluke. Lots of people knew about it.

Capezzi shook his head, and Aldo went about the business of beefing up security.

Capezzi polished off the three pounds of grapes in fifteen minutes, then asked his button man, Tony, to make him a chocolate malted.

Then Capezzi sat down in front of the TV to watch the rest of the 76ers game.

As he watched, he tried to figure out who might be doing this. But it was hard. The simple fact was that he had enough enemies to fill Veterans Stadium.

There were lots of people out there who, never mind fucking up his trailer, wanted to fuck him up, to pay him back for whatever.

And besides this, there were the cops. Periodically, despite him trying to keep a low profile, they came after him. He could see them doing this.

He called to Tony, who was standing nearby.

"Get me a refill," he said, and handed Tony the empty one-quart mug.

These guys didn't sound like wise guys. More like crazies. The laughter told him. Crazy laughter. Just break his *cojones* for no reason.

Or maybe for the risk. Capezzi knew there were wise guy buffs, people who liked to hang around wise guys, be near them like movie stars. Maybe play games with them.

But he knew there *had* to be a reason—and if you could find out the reason, you could find out the guy.

He had a lot of people looking for them, including some contacts at the cops. They would find them. But when?

He thought about the old shack, and a little fire started in his belly. He had been made a laughingstock. That was bad. Could make people think he could be fucked with.

A half hour later, Capezzi felt better. The Sixers had beat the spread, and he had pulled in a hundred large. For the moment, it drove away his trials and tribulations.

CHAPTER 20

It was Stein's friend at the ATF who had told Frankenstein about the *Maria*.

"It's registered in Maria Longo's name," Johnson had told Stein, "one of Capezzi's married daughters, but it's really owned by Daddy. He doesn't want anybody knowing he owns a million-dollar yacht. And in case he's nailed in court sometime, we can't use RICO to seize it."

"Nice boat?" Stein had asked.

"This is a boat and a half," Johnson said. "It's over sixty feet long, cored fiberglass hull, and solid—not cored—wood furniture made from lots of different rare hardwoods. It's got low, sleek lines—a really beautiful boat. A couple of years ago they did a short piece on it in *Yachting* Magazine; they had no idea a wise guy owned it."

"Hmm."

"Why do you want to know about it?"

"Personal reasons," Stein said, and then made a decision he sensed was the right one. "Look, just forget this conversation, okay, Jack?"

"No problem," Johnson said, "no problem."

Later, when he told Piccolo what he had done, Frank went along with it.

"Hey, Howie, there's no way what we're going to do is not going to be public knowledge. I'd rather Johnson know why he should be quiet."

A half hour after they called Capezzi, Frankenstein arrived at the Canoe House Marina, driving by without stopping just to get a sense of how it was laid out and whether anyone was around.

It was a typical marina, a series of docks jutting out into the Schuylkill River. A variety of boats were moored to the docks.

The docks were poorly lit, just an occasional light on a pole. About two blocks away there was a pink neon sign flashing BAR jutting out from the corner of a building.

They drove down to within a block of the bar, then started back toward the marina.

They parked within a block of the marina and got out of the car.

Both men were dressed in work clothes; Stein carried an overnight bag.

On their sweep through the marina, neither Stein nor Piccolo had been able to spot the boat, though it should have been easy to see. How many million-dollar, low-slung, sixty-two-foot yachts could there be in the river?

They walked down the dock. To their left was a boathouse of some sort, and as they reached its end, they realized they hadn't seen the *Maria* because it had been perfectly blocked by the building.

It was anchored about seventy-five yards off the dock. Even with its sails furled it was a magnificent boat, brilliant white, the white showing even through the darkness.

"I wonder how much fucking blood that cost!" Piccolo said.

"A lot," Howie said.

There was no one around, and there was plenty of transportation: a couple of rowboats were moored to the dock.

"Let's do it," Piccolo said.

Two minutes later they had cut the cords holding an old rowboat to the dock, hoisted anchor, and were rowing—Howie doing the rowing—toward the *Maria*.

A few minutes later, they were on board, and it was obvious that they were alone.

"This is a helluva boat," Piccolo said.

Fifteen seconds later, they were downstairs. Everything smelled of wood, superexpensive polished mahogany finished to a gentle sheen.

"Helluva fucking boat," Piccolo said.

But they had no time to admire it.

Within twenty seconds Howie had the two-foot spade bit in the brace. He held it in position with his right arm while his left, his thunderfist arm, turned it with astonishing speed and power, driving the spade bit through the cored fiberglass hull.

"Do it to it!" Piccolo, standing by the bar, exhorted.

Two minutes later, they heard the first gurgle.

"Let's get the fuck out of here," Piccolo cackled, "we're on the *Titanic*!"

It took the *Maria* about fifteen minutes to submerge, and as dangerous as it was for Frankenstein to watch—and possibly be spotted—they couldn't help themselves.

They waited until the hull was completely under water and then, spontaneously, just as they had done when filling the trailer with sewage, they shot their arms to the sky and let loose with cackles and howls.

How sweet it was!

Chapter 21

The phone in Angelo Capezzi's home rang at seven o'clock in the morning.

After listening to the reporter on the phone for a minute, a sleepy-eyed Aldo held the phone in his hand as if it were something you scooped up with a shovel at the elephant house. Aldo did not like to give Mr. Capezzi bad news.

A minute later, Aldo was tapping on the door of Angelo Capezzi's bedroom and a sleepy-sounding Capezzi told him to enter. Aldo entered.

As usual, it smelled bad. Capezzi ate a lot of garlic and farted all night.

Lying on his back in the bed, Capezzi said:

"What is it?" He sounded annoyed.

"Uh . . . Mr. Capezzi," Aldo said, "there's a reporter from a newspaper on the phone. Wants to speak with you. Something about the *Maria*.

Capezzi's voice was suddenly awake.

"My daughter?"

"No, no. Your boat. The *Maria*."

"What about it?"

"I don't know exactly," said Aldo, who knew exactly. "Something about it being sunk."

Capezzi flicked on the light. He looked worse in the morning than he did during the rest of the day. Indeed, he looked like the room smelled.

He picked up an ornate phone from a small table next to the bed.

"Yeah," he said, then, "wait a minute."

He looked at Aldo.

"Hang up the phone, will you?"

Aldo was glad to get out of the room. He went into the kitchen, where he had picked up the phone, and hung up. As he did, he heard the reporter's voice going like a machine gun.

Aldo went into the living room and sat on the couch. He thought about how his guys were on the street for a while now, and how they weren't able to find the guys who were doing this. He wondered how mad Capezzi was. Sometimes he could do bad things to people who weren't getting results. He knew of at least two guys who had been whacked for just fucking up jobs. He could be a scary guy.

Three minutes later, Capezzi called him into his bedroom. When he got there, Capezzi spoke to him in Italian, and his normally low voice was a little high. Aldo knew he was at the upper end of being pissed. When he spoke high and in Italian, he was extremely dangerous.

"This guy told me that someone sunk the *Maria*. They got a call awhile ago. The cops went down there, checked it out. Someone did sink it: those same *putanas* who destroyed the shack."

"Sons of bitches," Aldo said.

"Get me McKenna," Capezzi said.

Chapter 22

Within an hour of seeing Spano, Lawless found out that he had a yellow sheet. Lawless picked it up from central communications and took it back to the stationhouse.

He went into the squad room, poured himself a cup of coffee, and sat down at one of the desks; he resisted the urge for a cigarette and examined it.

Vincent Louis Spano lived in a private home on Williamsbridge Road, near Pelham Bay Parkway, not far from where Lawless lived.

The yellow sheet was nothing to get agitated about. Spano had been collared twice for gambling and there had been a couple of other misdemeanors related to gambling activity.

He had, Lawless figured, a bad habit.

Spano had had some difficulty with the DMV, having been in two accidents over the past few years. His license had been suspended once for driving without insurance.

Lawless went over the information a couple of more times slowly, then got up from the desk and went over to the window.

He lit a cigarette.

A not very remarkable record. A few dings, but nothing major. He was obviously a gambler.

So what?

Lawless needed to know more. He wanted to get a better fix on Spano.

He went back to his desk, pulled out a small brown notebook from his sports jacket pocket, and leafed through it until he found the two numbers he needed.

The numbers were of contacts he had at credit offices. He called them, told them he was interested in learning what kind of credit history Spano had. The two contacts, Artie Ladner of TRW and Joe Meagher of Trans Union, promised to get back to him quickly.

Ladner got back to him first.

"He's got a history of credit problems," he said, "going back quite a while. He owes about five thousand dollars to various stores and has two judgments against him."

"I see."

"He *is* making some progress paying off things."

"What do you mean?"

"Two weeks ago he paid off a couple of liens the IRS had on his house."

"How much?"

"Sixty-five hundred."

"I wonder if the IRS was squeezing him."

"No," Ladner said, "I spoke with them. He was paying off around two hundred and fifty a month. He missed his last couple of payments, but they were still in the letter stage."

"What's that?"

"Form letters rattling their sabers about catching up on his payments."

"So," Lawless said, "this all happened in one week. He paid off eight grand."

"That's right."

"Anything else?"

"That's about it. Everything we see says this is a guy with money problems."

"Thanks, Artie," Lawless said. "I appreciate it."

"Be well, my friend."

Meagher called a half hour after Ladner. He told Lawless the same things Ladner had told him about Spano, but had not followed through with the IRS. He also told Lawless

Spano was divorced and had been with Social Services for sixteen years.

Ten minutes after Meagher called, some new business came in: a pusher had been thrown off a roof on Anthony Avenue, so Lawless only had a few minutes to think about Spano's money problems and the recent big cash payments.

What he did have time to wonder about was where Spano got the money from.

Chapter 23

Racanelli had been out of town—an annual DAs' convention in Chicago—but Lawless arranged to meet with him as soon as he got back. They met at Pop's, a restaurant in the Bay Ridge section of Brooklyn, which was clean and safe, not unlike Arthur Avenue.

Pop's had good food and drink at reasonable prices, and old-fashioned charm and manners. It was a well-known watering hole for law enforcement people. Legend had it that one day in the mid-seventies two junkies had come in and tried to heist the place and were subdued by the instant appearance of seventeen handguns, three shotguns, two rifles, an alley gun, an Uzi, and a heat-seeking atomic warhead.

It was said that more cases were settled over lasagna at Pop's than in courtrooms.

Though it was midnight—and a weekday—when Lawless came in, the place was crowded.

Racanelli was sitting alone in a booth in the back, but his bodyguards were eating at a nearby table.

They eyed Lawless as he moved in Racanelli's direction, but they knew him and just nodded as he slipped into the booth opposite Racanelli.

Racanelli had a plate of raw vegetables in front of him, also a large bottle of San Pellegrino sparkling water.

"Want something, Joe?"

"Just water."

"Pellegrino or water?"

"Pellegrino."

Racanelli turned a glass over and placed it in front of Lawless. He poured the glass full of water, then pushed a small dish containing lemon and lime wedges toward Lawless. Lawless dropped a lime into the water.

"There are very few things in Pop's I can eat," Racanelli said. "This is cholesterol country."

Lawless smiled. These days most guys with Ono's job would be more concerned about walking on the street than their cholesterol count.

Racanelli took a bite of raw asparagus.

"How's it going?" Lawless asked.

"Not much progress with Pran," Racanelli said, referring to the slumlord of the Miramar. "He's been out of town—and his lawyer said he was out of town when Irmgard was killed."

"Which proves nothing," Lawless said.

Racanelli nodded.

"Yeah. What's happening with Spano?"

Spano was the purpose of the meeting. Lawless told him about the yellow sheet and the credit problems. And the apparent sudden infusion of money to pay off the IRS.

"What do you make of it? Can you tie it to Irmgard?"

"Not yet. It's just that there's *stuff* going on in his life that can't be explained. He was in contact with Werner—and he lied. We question him, he runs to a lawyer. Now, he suddenly has money."

Racanelli chewed on an asparagus; Lawless sipped the water.

"I come back to the same thing," Racanelli said.

Lawless nodded.

"The question is what do we do next?"

Lawless nodded.

"I think," Lawless said, "we should crunch him a little. Tell him we know the story. Maybe we can fake him out. I don't think he's that tough."

"That might be the best way," Racanelli said, "if he's gotten a lawyer . . ."

"I can tell him I want to discuss it without the lawyer, off the record. Imply we want to deal. But if the lawyer is in it, all bets are off."

Racanelli said nothing.

"It's worth a whack," Lawless said.

Racanelli washed the asparagus down with a long sip of water.

"Okay. Just keep it legal."

The slightest of smiles played around Lawless's mouth.

"We only use UL rated cattle prods," Lawless said.

Chapter 24

Lawless learned that Spano started work at eight A.M. He figured that if he began the surveillance on Spano's house at six-thirty, he would be there when Spano left for work.

Williamsbridge Road, where Spano lived, ran into Pelham Bay Parkway, a broad avenue that ran east and west across the Bronx, where Lawless lived.

It took Lawless less than five minutes to drive to Spano's home, which was a private house.

There were very few parking spaces on the street, but he was able to squeeze his battered, white 1964 Impala into a space about fifty yards down from Spano's house.

As soon as he did, he slid over into the passenger seat. It was an old trick. If anyone noticed him, they would assume he was a passenger waiting for the driver.

The street was typically middle class and in good condition. Red- and cream-colored brick apartment buildings were interspersed on both sides of the street with private homes.

Spano's house, like the others, was two stories, flat roofed, shingled, and had a porch that led to glass doors. A few yards to the right of the house was a single-car, peaked-roof garage. A short Cyclone fence ran across the front of the property.

It did not vary much from the other homes on the block, except it seemed in worse shape. It needed a paint job, and the roof on both the house and the free-standing garage looked as if they needed to be replaced.

It definitely did not look like the home of a rich man.

A couple of times Lawless resisted the urge to smoke.

By seven, as far as he could tell, there had not been any activity inside Spano's house.

As he waited, Lawless jotted down the license plate numbers of all the cars on the street he could see from the car. Later, he would run them through the DMV to see what, if anything, they could tell him. It was a practice that could bear fruit. It also helped relieve the boredom.

One cop he once knew had a terrifically high felony arrest record because he had a photographic memory, and used it to record license plate numbers. It was surprising the kinds of relationships and connections you could find.

By seven-fifteen traffic had increased. Spano worked on

Southern Boulevard. If he wanted to get there by eight, he'd have to be leaving the house soon.

A number of people had walked their dogs. That, he thought, was better than them walking themselves. Over the past few years more and more people, mostly cabdrivers but upstanding types as well, were urinating in the streets. He had collared one cab driver. It was a nothing offense, but you couldn't let people act like pigs.

He noticed a woman walking a dog in the direction of Spano's house. She was middle-aged, had curly red hair. The dog was a brown Lab.

The dog paused and urinated at the curb, then she continued in the direction of the house.

She stopped by the curb opposite Spano's house, and Lawless waited for the dog to finish doing her business.

But she didn't, and Lawless realized that it was the woman who had stopped for something. She was looking at Spano's house. Lawless tried to follow her line of sight. What was she looking at?

He scanned the house.

There was a porch, four windows on top, three lower windows. All were curtained or had shades. He doubted she could see in them.

His eyes traced the flat roofline of the house, then the garage.

He kept trying to calculate the angle the woman was looking at. It was hard, except she kept looking to the right, either at the right side of the house or maybe the garage. The garage didn't have a window. What could she see?

After perhaps thirty seconds the woman moved on in the direction she had come from. She seemed to be moving faster than she had when she first came down the block.

Lawless wondered what to do. Maybe just go up and knock on the door. But some of the element of surprise would be lost. He wanted to hit him hard and fast.

He felt the urge for a cigarette.

He pulled a pack of Carltons from his inside breast pocket and went through the ritual of turning back the foil that covered the opening he had made.

He tapped a cigarette out, then pulled out his lighter. Then he changed his mind. He put the cigarettes and lighter away.

Over the next few minutes, traffic increased even more. The day was starting in earnest.

Lawless thought it was going to be a nice one. Since dawn—he had gotten up at five—the sky had been mottled gray and white, mostly gray. Now the sun had burned through and the sky was powder blue, most clouds gone.

Lawless's eyes flicked to the right. He turned. Across the street the same woman who had walked the dog was walking down the block in the direction of Spano's house. This time she didn't have the dog with her.

She was moving rather quickly. Her expression was distressed and her body language beamed the message that she was agitated.

Lawless watched her intently.

As he knew she would, she turned in at Spano's house, letting herself in through the gate, glancing at the garage on the right as she climbed the porch steps.

She pressed the bell and waited.

After fifteen seconds, she pressed the bell again.

Nothing.

Twenty seconds after this, she went down the steps and followed a short concrete path to the driveway, two concrete strips flanking a strip of grass. She walked down it.

She came to a stop a few yards in front of the garage door and just looked. He sensed she was very upset. What the hell was going on?

Then, suddenly, she was moving away from the garage door, and even from across the street Lawless could tell she was white.

He got out of the car. She had just passed out of the gate when she saw him.

He flashed his tin; simultaneously he heard the *putt-putt* of an engine.

"Thank God," she said. "I'm worried about the person who lives in here. There's no answer, and I think there's a car running *inside* the garage."

"Wait here," Lawless said.

Lawless went through the gate, over to the garage.

There *was* a motor running—and when you got close, there was the smell of exhaust.

He tried the door handle. It was open.

He pulled the garage door up and then tried to leap out of the way as exhaust billowed out, enveloping him.

Chapter 25

Vic Onairuts, the ME, who occasionally showed a warped and cynical sense of humor, said at the scene that Vincent Spano had been "parboiled."

Spano was lying on his left side in the backseat of his car, a gray 1979 Buick LeSabre in less-than-mint condition.

He had friction fit a vacuum cleaner hose over the end of the tail pipe, then had fed the hose through the rear window, closed the window against the hose to hold it in place, closed the other windows (or they were already closed), and turned the car on.

The "parboiled" description came from the condition of Spano's skin. Normally in a CO death, the skin is rosy red, pinkish—the victim actually looks very healthy.

But when the body is subject to hot exhaust gases for an

extended period of time—a couple of hours—the skin can turn cherry red, almost cooked. Indeed, Spano's body temperature was 117 degrees.

Onairuts told Lawless that he figured Spano was dead at least three hours, but both men knew that this was an estimate. Determining precisely when someone died was the stuff movies were made of.

The scene, Lawless thought, was a classic CO suicide scene.

The car radio was on, in this case tuned to 106.7 FM, a station that played oldies and very soft rock.

To make the garage as airtight as possible, Spano had stuffed toweling into a narrow space between the bottom of the garage door and the concrete floor.

Spano—also not uncommon—had been drinking, probably heavily.

Lawless and two crime scene people found a fifth of Cutty Sark about three-quarters empty on the kitchen table in the house.

There was no note, which was also not unusual, or any other indication of why he killed himself. Lawless also checked for a VCR, because he had once run into a suicide who had a teary farewell on tape.

None.

Spano's fiscal problems were reflected in his car, also the furniture and furnishings. Lawless had walked through every room on both floors: it looked as if the furniture had been bought from the Salvation Army. It had that certain battered look, with no consistency of style from piece to piece.

The rooms needed a paint job as badly as the station house.

Still, Lawless wasn't convinced it was suicide.

Racanelli, who had been in court, joined Lawless at around noon.

After checking out the scene Racanelli suggested they

take a walk. They headed down Williamsbridge Road, toward Pelham Bay Parkway.

"What do you think?" Racanelli said.

"It only makes it more of a mystery for me. Why would he kill himself? It doesn't make a lot of sense to pay off the IRS one week and kill yourself the next."

"I agree. So what do you think?"

"Maybe he had some help."

"Anything concrete?"

"No. But—"

Racanelli interrupted.

"But when we talked with him, he wasn't acting like a man who was depressed enough to kill himself."

"That's right. He was too aggressive."

"Of course, there's really no foolproof way to predict when someone is going to kill himself."

Lawless nodded.

They had reached Pelham Bay Parkway and now turned around.

"I'll just have to keep digging," Lawless said.

CHAPTER 26

Leo McKenna and Angelo Capezzi had something in common: both were obese, though McKenna was not nearly as large as Capezzi. Then again, few living things were as large as Capezzi.

Like Capezzi, McKenna liked Italian food, Chinese food, Indian food, American food—food in very large portions and at all hours of the day or night.

Unlike Capezzi, who would have only an occasional glass

of vino, McKenna liked to drink. He was fifty-nine and could not drink like he used to, but he could still put away, as he would playfully say, an occasional "jeriboam or balthazar of brew." When someone would ask what they were, he would delight in defining what the sizes were.

Also unlike Capezzi, McKenna was not physically repulsive. He was nice-looking, with a shock of whitish hair, twinkling blue eyes, a reddish face, nice features, and a quick smile.

Like Capezzi, McKenna was a very nasty individual.

McKenna drank during his entire time on the job in the N.Y.P.D. He figured the IAD freaks would eventually get to him for past transgressions, so he drank to take the edge off; he had an edge on during all his waking hours.

McKenna mostly drank alone, or with one of the various girlfriends he had, or a cop or two who, like him, had to be dirty—so dirty it wouldn't pay to flip.

With McKenna, it had never been a case of burnout turning him dirty.

McKenna was dirty from the start, and even as he sat in DeWitt Clinton High School in the Bronx on one hot summer day in 1957 taking the test for the department, he was wondering just how much money the shield would allow him to steal. His father had been a cop before him and, though a patrolman for all his time on the job, he always lived high on the hog. For little Leo it was simply a case of like father like son.

IAD had tried to bring the hammer down on him on three separate occasions, but they'd failed. He was smart and careful and cynical to a fault. He once told one of his girlfriends that before saying anything incriminating to anyone he would strip search them. "That includes mymother." From the way he said it, she wondered if he was kidding.

IAD always knew he was dirty, some superiors knew he was dirty, but no one could nail him. During his twenty years on the job, he was transferred to so many different precincts—CO's just didn't like a cop like him around—you'd think he had the plague.

But the promise of the job fulfilled itself. He made a truck full of dirty money, and he knew how to collect and hide it. And most of the time he lived well within his means, though when he knew he could get away with it, he would hit Las Vegas for a night on the strip. He would never be caught in what cops called a "net worth" investigation, where wrongdoing can be proven when a cop's life-style exceeds his income. He banked the dirty money in Switzerland and the Bahamas. He figured he would let it all hang out after he threw in his papers, which was the way it happened.

Getting mobbed up was a natural extension of his activities. He had been working for Angelo Capezzi now for seven years.

Their relationship had been very ordinary, until Frankie Parente came along.

Capezzi had hired McKenna to find out if Parente, who had wiled his way into Capezzi's family, was a UC.

McKenna had found out that Parente's real name was Frankie Vano and he was an N.Y.P.D. narc attached to DEA.

One day, very quietly so that the cops could never be sure Capezzi did it, Vano/Parente was killed; his body was never recovered.

Capezzi was very grateful to McKenna for that and paid him ten large. Maybe even more important, his respect for McKenna's investigative abilities skyrocketed. So whenever he had a special job going, he would call him.

His most recent one, worth seven and a half large, was finding out about the Ferret, the little snitch who was working with some cops to bring a Capezzi chop shop operation down.

McKenna had learned that they'd just come up with his body. That was a fuckup of the first order. Wops were so dumb they couldn't even get rid of a body.

McKenna thought it was lucky it wasn't the DEA guy; then balls would have been broken. But it was just a snitch.

McKenna met Capezzi in an italian restaurant named The Silver Grotto in downtown Camden, N.J., the evening of the same day the reporter called Capezzi about the *Maria*.

They took dinner in a private room in the back, working their way through course after delicious course of food as they talked about this and that and finally got around to Capezzi's current difficulties.

"These guys are trying to make an asshole of me," Capezzi said as he unloaded a forkful of pasta with sundried tomatoes into his mouth, "and that can't happen. You let something like that go, people think you're getting soft; they don't try to take your boat or trailer out, they take you out."

He munched methodically. McKenna eyed him. He was a loathesome fat pig of a wop, but he was smart. McKenna knew that if he ever got on the wrong side of this pig, he would have his hands full.

"If I find 'em," McKenna asked, "what do you want me to do?"

Capezzi took a long sip of red wine, loaded his fork up again.

"Just tell me who they are. We'll take it from there."

McKenna loaded his own fork with a hunk of lamb shank and filled his mouth so that he could not speak.

"The job is worth twelve large," Capezzi said.

McKenna was the master of various faces, but he almost choked on the lamb when Capezzi named the figure. He had just offered him more large than he'd paid for the UC.

He chewed slowly and deliberately; he'd rather choke to death than have Capezzi do the Heimlich on him. He swallowed and said softly:

"Same expense money?"

"No," Capezzi said, "fifty dollars more a day."

"That sounds fine."

Capezzi looked at him and sipped the wine, his little pig eyes glittering.

McKenna thought that when he found these guys he would love to be the beneficiary of any life insurance policies they had.

Chapter 27

McKenna conducted the investigation like he would any squeal. You start at the point where the crime occurred and work outward.

In this case, it was the trailer—or where the trailer had been. The one that was destroyed had been replaced by a new one.

The day after he had talked to Capezzi, he started schlepping up and down Penrose Street, going into junkyards, refinery yards, and other places on the street, talking to personnel to see if anyone had seen anything.

McKenna did not care where Capezzi's button men had gone. For one thing, he conducted his own investigation. For another, he had no faith whatsoever in the button men. Capezzi was a smart wop, but button men, as a rule, were just a bunch of dumb guineas; the most complicated thing they could handle was a Louisville Slugger.

Money greased the wheels. As he went, McKenna would hand out five- and ten-dollar bills to anyone who talked with him, even if they didn't provide any leads. He had long ago found out that when you handed out money, people tended to remember you—and would strive to remember things they had forgot.

It took him two days to work his way up and down Penrose.

The dumping, as he thought of it, had occurred sometime in the wee hours of Sunday morning, which could be considered good or bad. Bad because the wee hours of the morning wasn't a time when witnesses were falling out of the trees, and good because any witness would be likely to notice any unusual activity. And pumping three thousand gallons of shit into a trailer was an unusual activity.

McKenna had made a call to a friend in the Health Department and found out that to dump three thousand gallons of sewage, at the rate of eighty to one hundred gallons a minute, meant that the dudes were on the scene at least a half hour. Somebody should have seen them.

And what balls it took. To stay that long doing that to someone like Capezzi. They had to be a little crazy.

By the end of the second day, despite high hopes and liberal cash distribution, McKenna had not found anyone who saw anything.

At the start of the third day of his investigation, he struck out in another area: with the cops. He knew a PI who was an ex-Philly cop, and McKenna asked him to make some inquiries for him at the Philly PD. The Philly cops had no idea who the perps were and, more to the point, didn't care.

"You know," McKenna's contact said, "the Philly cops have no love for Capezzi. One of them said they only wished Capezzi was in the trailer instead of the dog when the shit came in. It's not that simple to get cooperation."

McKenna shelled out an additional large to get people to swallow their feelings about Capezzi and to think again. Money was not only a grease but a salve.

On the evening of the fourth day, a Friday, McKenna, as much as he disliked it, went on stakeout across the street from where the new trailer was.

No matter how much surveillance work he had done on the job, nothing could make it any easier. It was a pain in the ass. Literally. Just sit in the car, smoking, eating, drinking, smelling your own farts, watching the dark, deserted street for someone who might have seen something.

It was confirmed to McKenna that Penrose was not a main traffic artery of Philadelphia. There would be an occasional passenger car or delivery truck, but nothing stopped, except when the streetlights, far down the broad block, turned red.

Once someone did stop across the street and maybe fifty yards down from the trailer. It was an old, battered, hardtop convertible and, as it turned in before parking on the street, he got a glimpse of two figures silhouetted in the front—a driver and someone in the passenger seat.

He waited until the car was parked a few minutes, then quietly got out of his car and approached it.

When he was within ten yards he knew why the car had parked. He could see it moving rhythmically ever so slightly.

He went back to his own car and gave the lovers another five minutes to finish off, then he started the car, pulled out into Penrose, and brought it to a stop just to the rear of the hardtop.

Then he went to the rear window and tapped on the glass. There was scuffling inside the car, then the front door opened up and a big nigger got out. McKenna flashed a phony shield.

The body language of the nigger had spelled trouble when he first got out, but he softened when he saw the shield.

"Sorry to bother you," McKenna said, "but I was wondering if you were here last Sunday night."

"No."

"Oh," McKenna said, "we're trying to get a line on who vandalized the trailer over there." He pointed to it.

"Don't know nothing about it."

"How about your girlfriend?"

"No, she don't know nothing, neither."

McKenna was in sort of a nasty mood from sitting. He pressed it.

"Ask her to get out of the car."

The nigger hesitated, but then complied.

A curvaceous nigger woman got out, and McKenna asked her the same question.

The answer was the same: she didn't see nothing.

McKenna nodded, got into his car, and drove back to his position across the street. A minute later the hardtop took off.

He would have liked to arrange to fuck the nigger, but he had to stay on the job.

On Sunday night, McKenna figured he had his best shot. It was a week to the day that the shack was hit. Hopefully somebody would have happened along while the truck was dumping.

Traffic early Sunday night was even thinner than on the other days. McKenna figured he knew where almost everyone was: home watching TV. That's what almost everybody did on Sunday night, which is why it was the best time to serve a warrant, whatever the offense. Perps watched TV on Sunday night, too.

Occasionally a truck would lumber by and McKenna would jot down the license plate number. He would feed these numbers to his PI contact, who would get them run through the Pennsylvania Motor Vehicle Department. Then McKenna would get on the horn and find out who the drivers were and talk with them.

He got the number of a meat truck, a milk truck, one carrying live fowl, and a newspaper delivery truck.

Three cabs passed along Penrose during the night, all

from different companies. He wrote the plates down anyway. If he had to, he would check with the dispatchers to see if any of the company's cabs were in the area at the right time.

McKenna had also set up a snitch network with his contact, but he seriously doubted they'd come up with anything. Capezzi had snitches everywhere, and if he hadn't come up with anything, how would McKenna?

McKenna left at dawn. He was not surprised that so far there were no leads. That was par for the course. Back when he was on the job, it was par for the course, too. Back then, though, he had another twenty-four thousand people helping.

But he had himself, and that was worth something.

CHAPTER 28

Frankenstein was on a four-to-eight. It was now two in the afternoon, two days after the media had informed Capezzi that his "daughter's" yacht was on the bottom of the Schuylkill River.

Frankenstein was sitting at the kitchen table in their apartment. Between them was a bottle of guinea red. Piccolo was sipping the guinea red, Stein had San Pellegrino mineral water.

The weather had turned cold, but in the kitchen it was warm and sunny. Both men were feeling very mellow, more than partially fulfilled by the consternation they were causing Capezzi. Again, the action had made it up front in both the *Philadelphia Daily News* and the *Enquirer*, and Stein's friend Johnson had called and told Stein he only had one thing to say:

"Ha, ha!"

Piccolo took a gulp of wine from his water glass.

"When I was in "Nam," he said, "I met a little guy named Preston. Tough little son of a bitch, out of Salt Lake City.

"Like me, he was a tunnel rat," Piccolo continued, referring to the job that was arguably the worst in Vietnam and involved crawling down rat-and-spider-infested tunnels to go one on one in the darkness with the VC, "and we used to talk a lot. I don't remember everything he said, but I do remember one thing in particular."

"What's that?"

"He said, 'Frank, if you're going to break balls, break balls. I mean, like, don't stop. Just keep breaking them. Don't go halfway.' "

"I don't exactly understand what he meant," Stein said.

"Neither did I—or do I," Piccolo said, "but I know this. I think we should apply Preston's philosophy to Jabba the Hutt. I think we should squeeze his balls until our fingers go through them like overripe fucking melons."

"If we do that," Howie said, "he's definitely going to come after us—assuming he's not after us now."

"He don't know who's doing this shit to him. That's a big advantage."

"So, you want to try to come up with another idea?"

"Sure. Maybe," Piccolo said, "we'll fucking torch his house—with him in it. Nothing nasty."

Stein laughed. He volunteered an idea.

"Maybe we could get into his home in some way. Make his cesspool overflow."

"I love it, but it's too tough. He must have goons all over the joint by now."

Stein felt himself getting swept up into the spirit of things. He took a long, delicate sip with his thunderfist arm. Piccolo thought it was like watching Popeye.

"How about," Stein said, "dropping a couple of rounds of mortar on the house?"

Piccolo smiled broadly and cackled.

"I like that!"

Piccolo took another drink. This was fun.

"Maybe," he said, "we could find out where his kids are. Kill them. Ship them to a meat factory and have them ground up into fucking sausage. Then ship them to Capezzi with a little note explaining what he's received. *C-O* fucking *D!*"

Piccolo cackled, and Stein howled. After they settled down, Stein presented another idea.

"Is his wife alive?"

They laughed again. They were getting giddy.

"Let's see if we can get someone in the Air Force to drop an atom bomb on his house," Stein said.

"Make it an H bomb," Piccolo said.

They laughed heartily.

Piccolo took another sip of the wine. He held up a finger.

"What about," he said, "germ warfare?"

"I got it," Stein said. "We'll hire someone with AIDS to have anal intercourse with Capezzi!"

"I love it!" Piccolo said. "What a way to go. And as he's on his last legs, we can then make the cesspool overflow!"

They howled, tittered, cackled.

They clinked glasses. Piccolo refilled his, then Stein's.

Piccolo looked at Stein. He was, he thought, a good guy. Real. And a Jew. A touch Jew, not a pussy. Nobody was tougher than a tough Jew. He was so lucky to have someone like him, and for a millisecond a chill passed through him. He pushed the thought out of his mind.

They sat silently for a while.

"You know we're going to think of something else, right?" Piccolo asked.

"Oh, yeah," Stein answered. "Something more realistic than an H bomb."

"But just as painful," Piccolo said, and they laughed some more.

Chapter 29

Another week had gone by in the Werner case, and Lawless, though he had not spent all his time on it, had spent quite a bit, and he was still at a dead end.

He decided to do what he often did when cases weren't working out: he would revisit the crime scene. Sometimes taking a fresh look at a scene would bring insights that you didn't have the first time around.

Here, he had two scenes to visit. He drove over to Spano's house around nine A.M.; it was raining. He parked directly opposite the house.

The house looked ordinary. The crime scene tape was gone, and the uniformed cops had been reassigned.

As he recalled the events of that day, he also focused on some of the facts the investigation had thus far revealed.

Spano had drank a huge amount of booze. His blood-alcohol level was 3.8; 4.0 was considered a lethal amount.

"It's a wonder," Onairuts had said, "that he could make it from the house to the car."

Lawless wondered if he'd had some help.

There were no usable prints found on the car; except for Spano's, all the others were smudged.

Spano was in fairly good health, with a normal body for a man his age, Onairuts had said.

Lawless had had a conversation with Spano's supervisor and he had told him that, as far as he knew, Spano was not an alcoholic.

That was borne out by tests on his liver. It showed no cirrhosis or other damage associated with drinking.

Which would make his getting bombed like he did very unusual. Then again, killing yourself had to be counted as an unusual event in anyone's life.

The supervisor *did* confirm that Spano was a heavy gambler and that he, the supervisor, had been called a number of times by his creditors. The supervisor had said he'd warned Spano that his job could be in jeopardy if he kept on gambling, but that Spano wasn't worried that much; he knew how strong the city unions were.

Lawless got out of the car, went across the street, and entered the house with one of Spano's keys.

It took Lawless only five minutes to walk the rooms; it left him with no new insights.

Financially there had been one fresh detail learned over the last week: up until two weeks ago, he had been in default—three months—on the house mortgage, but had paid fifteen hundred dollars in arrears to catch up.

That meant he had shelled out almost eight grand in a couple of weeks. Where was the money coming from?

Lawless stood next to the kitchen table where they had found the almost empty bottle of scotch.

Lawless exited the house from the back sun porch door and walked around, opened the garage door with another key, and pulled it up.

He stepped inside.

The car was gone, impounded, but the smell of exhaust was still there.

He walked around the garage.

Nothing unusual. Some old gardening tools hanging on nails on the walls, a couple of shelves with cans of paint from the year of the flood.

Lawless pulled the garage door down, locked it, walked around to the sun porch, and back into the kitchen. It was, he estimated, about a thirty-yard walk. A long walk if Spano was as inebriated as he should have been.

Lawless left by the front door, locking it behind him.

As it happened, Lawless couldn't even think of going to the Miramar until that night. There had been a vicious killing on Creston Avenue: an old Jewish guy had been bound, gagged, robbed, and beaten to death.

It was the kind of crime, Lawless thought, that you got relatively often in the Five Three. It went beyond robbery. The perps were just waiting to unload their rage on some helpless old man or woman.

He finally got to the Miramar at ten at night. The rain had stopped falling while he was at Spano's, but it was cold, the kind of day that gave a real hint of winter.

He found a space about fifty yards from Irmgard's house and parked. He got out of the car and started walking toward the building.

Lawless knew many of the street people figured him for a cop. Otherwise, what was a blond-haired white man doing on the Grand Concourse at night? Either he was a cop or a drug customer, and dealers knew their customers by heart.

As he walked along, he could see the effect his presence had.

Two Hispanics leaning against a car maybe fifty yards beyond the entrance of Irmgard's building moved away. A cluster of black dudes across the street had also started to slowly amble away.

Lawless acted oblivious to it all and turned into the building.

Like Spano's, the crime scene tape had been removed. It was business as usual.

The super was in apartment 1A. Lawless rang the bell which, incongruously, chimed inside. A minute later the door opened. The super was a big black guy with a pot belly and a balding, shiny dome. He recognized Lawless right away.

"Yes, sir?"

"How you doing, Mr. Gaines?"

"Okay."

"I'd like to take a look at Ms. Werner's apartment again."

The super's face screwed up.

"Somebody moved in there a week ago."

"They there now?"

"Don't know."

"Maybe they'll let me look anyway."

The super nodded and stepped out into the lobby. Lawless followed him across the lobby to the apartment where Irmgard Werner had lived.

Lawless could hear music coming from inside the apartment.

The super knocked.

"Mr. Leibowitz?"

It took a little Q and A between the super and Liebowitz before the door was opened.

He was an old man, small, bespectacled. Lawless figured him to be in his seventies.

"Mr. Liebowitz," Lawless said before the super could talk, "I'd like to take a look at your room."

"Why?"

"I'm with Social Services," Lawless said, glancing at Gaines, "and I just want to make sure everything is okay."

The old man nodded.

"Come in," he said.

The man stepped aside and Lawless followed the super into the room. The old man closed the door behind them.

Lawless stopped a few feet inside the door and surveyed the room.

The furniture, what there was of it—bed, dresser, table, and lamp next to the bed—were in the same positions as when Irmgard lived there, but the room had a completely different feeling.

The old man had hung some black-and-white pictures of some woman and kids that probably were taken forty or fifty years earlier. The holy pictures had been taken down.

The bedspread was different, and there was an old-fashioned radio on the table that was tuned to a station that was playing Yiddish music.

The room simply had the feeling of an old person, different from the feminine feeling he got when Irmgard lived there.

But Lawless could picture the crime scene.

Irmgard Werner's body lying facedown on the floor, fully dressed, her blouse bloody, throat cut, blue eyes fixed and dilated, her hands by her sides, her legs spread slightly.

The dresser drawers were open, clothing in the closet in a pile on the floor, the mattress half hanging off the bed. The killer had been searching for something. The white bedspread had been spattered with blood, teardropped shaped blood spatters were on the wall.

Things were all over the floor.

The window opened.

A classic crime scene. The very phrase bothered him.

He walked around the room, asked Mr. Leibowitz a few harmless questions about whether he was satisfied or not. Mr. Leibowitz said he was.

Lawless thanked him, and then he and Gaines left.

"Thanks," Lawless said, "for going along with me. I didn't see any point in scaring the old guy."

"No problem," Gaines said.

* * *

As he drove back to the station, Lawless thought about the crime scene at the Miramar and then, without realizing it, he found himself thinking about the Spano scene.

He felt like a cigarette and this time lit up. He dragged deeply. There was a little guilt, but a lot more pleasure.

He kept picturing both crime scenes. He remembered what Onairuts had said about both cases. He remembered Ono's observations, what the crime scene guys said.

There was something there, inside him, but he couldn't remember it.

He parked the car on the street near the station house, entered the building, and was halfway up the stairs to the squad room when the insight hit him, literally stopped him in his tracks. He went up the rest of the stairs two at a time.

CHAPTER 30

Lawless was going to call Racanelli as soon as he got back to the squad room. As it happened, Racanelli had called him—twice.

Lawless called and got right through.

"Joe, thanks for calling back. I located Dr. Bloom."

"When? How?"

"The Social Service mud sheets," Racanelli said. "I just got my copies a little while ago."

"I found that Spano not only called Irmgard a few times on the hotel phone, but I noticed that both of them had called the same number fairly frequently," Racanelli said. "And it's our mysterious friend Dr. Bloom.

"I found out that Spano called Bloom just a few minutes after we hit him that day."

"What's Spano doing talking to Irmgard's boyfriend?"

"That's precisely what I want to know, Joe."

"What's next?"

"I called the number. It's an answering service. He's a psychologist. I didn't leave a message. I want you to move in on this."

"No problem. What's the number?"

Racanelli gave it to him. Then:

"And what did you have?"

"It pales by comparison," Lawless said, "and it's only a theory. I think Spano was murdered."

"How so?"

"The thing that kept bugging me was that the scenes were so perfect. The thing is they're *too* perfect."

"It would take someone with experience to do it. Like a cop."

"Precisely."

There was a silence.

"Okay," Lawless said, "I'll get on it right away."

"One other thing, Joe," Racanelli said, "Pran, the Miramar landlord—he's got an airtight alibi. More important, though, is he struck me as being innocent. I'm going to exclude him unless something else comes in."

"Okay."

"Good luck, Joe."

After they hung up, Racanelli thought about the possibility that someone in law enforcement might be involved. To him, other than murder, that was the most loathsome crime of all.

But it was just a theory.

On the other hand, it was Lawless's theory, and he wasn't just another cop.

Racanelli forced his mind back to the work at hand. But

he found it hard. The whole case smelled of conspiracy. By who? And why?

CHAPTER 31

In the ten days that he had been on the case, McKenna had spent most of his time pursuing leads, if you could call them that, that developed from his stakeout of Penrose Street.

There was really only one that yielded solid information. A guy driving a newspaper delivery truck remembered seeing a truck that looked as if it might be a cesspool truck—it had a big tubular tank—parked near the trailer.

And he remembered the smell.

"It smelled very bad. I had to turn up the windows. I thought they were pumping stuff out, not in."

McKenna gave the guy twenty dollars and questioned him very closely.

Did the truck have any markings?

The driver didn't think it had any.

Could he remember the license plate, or any part of it?

No, it was very dark.

How about the driver? Worker?

Yes, he remembered a guy on the roof of the trailer. He couldn't give any description at all, except that the guy was big.

Sounds?

Yes, the sound of the truck—and he thought he heard a dog barking.

The driver was also able to fix the time at three thirty-five

A.M., which was only a few minutes after he left the KM Stationary Store on Kline, which he usually hit at three-thirty.

But that was it.

The snitch network, predictably, had not yielded anything. And no one was getting back to him from all the interrogations he had done on the street.

McKenna told Capezzi softly yet clearly that he was getting nowhere with the Penrose case, as he put it, and he could tell that Capezzi wasn't happy. McKenna tried to assuage what he felt Capezzi was feeling by telling him that things weren't dead yet, but he was not overly optimistic. You didn't want to give a wop wise guy like Capezzi false hope.

He decided to switch his investigation to the sinking of the *Maria*. If anything developed with the Penrose job, it developed.

One of Capezzi's button men showed McKenna where the *Maria* had been anchored, and then McKenna spent an entire day walking the area and asking questions. He talked with the owner and patrons of a bar located down the street from where the boat was anchored, a guy who owned a bait and tackle shop, another guy who owned a food store.

Also, there were a number of businesses in streets leading to the area where the ships were anchored and he talked to a lot of the people who worked in them. There were also a couple of small apartment buildings, one empty, and McKenna talked to some of the tenants there.

The problem, McKenna determined, was simple: while there were people around who might have seen something during the day, the place turned into a virtual wasteland at night.

It was the same kind of problem he had at Penrose.

After two days of questioning people, McKenna took the same tack as on Penrose. He put the marina area under surveillance, parking his car a block away from the pier, near where the *Maria* had been moored.

As he sat there the first night, watching, writing down license plate numbers, he realized that the guys who did this job had the pedigree to attack again. It was just a question of when. He hoped he could nail them before they did. He didn't like dealing with Capezzi when he was super pissed, and if he didn't find them soon, that was sure to fucking happen.

Chapter 32

Frankenstein, like most cop partners, was getting to the point where verbal communication was, in many instances, unnecessary. They each knew what the other was thinking.

A prime example of this kind of communication showed itself when they were called to the Blue Moon Diner on 182nd Street and Ryer Avenue to investigate a burglary.

The Blue Moon was in "Death Valley," the worst part of Fort Siberia, and run by two very stubborn Greek brothers. Frankenstein and other squad members had been there numerous times. The diner was broken into by junkies an astonishing average of three times a month, and they stole anything that wasn't bolted to the floor. Indeed, the flooring—wide oak planks—was stolen the second or third time the place was hit.

The brothers, whose name was Onassis—no relation—were often asked by patrons and police why they just didn't close the place down.

The response was simple and in Greek: "Fuck 'em."

In the old days, the sixties, the cops would have staked out the place, put a shotgun team out of sight, and waited for perps. But those days were gone.

Shotgun teams had better things to do, and even if they didn't it probably wouldn't do any good: perps in the precinct routinely risked their lives for crack.

At any rate, Frankenstein had completed the investigation, had gotten back into their car for the trip to the station, when Piccolo said, as if they were in the midst of a conversation:

"While we're trying to come up with a good way to break his balls some more, I was thinking that we could do a few little things in the meantime."

"I was thinking, too," Stein said, "that we could make some calls and order some things for him."

"Yeah," Piccolo said, "magazines and the like."

"We'll look into it," Stein said, "see what we can come up with."

Back at the station, in the squad room, Stein typed up the DD5 report—using, as usual, only his thunderfist hand and cranking along at seventy wpm—and Piccolo began the research, starting with the Yellow Pages for ideas.

As soon as he was finished with the report, Stein joined him; it soon became clear the fill-in ballbreaking might be a little more time consuming than they'd originally thought. It was not the kind of thing they should be doing on the job. That wouldn't be fair to the job or to Lawless, the squad commander, who Frankenstein liked. Or to Capezzi.

They waited until they got to their apartment before starting the researching in earnest.

The first idea was to order fag magazines in Capezzi's name. Said Piccolo:

"See if we can get himself subscriptions to things like *Black Stud* and *Golden Rod,* have some of his buttons wonder if he's chowing down on little boys or taking it up the chocolate speedway."

But the flaw was that subscriptions took weeks, maybe months, to arrive. Frankenstein wanted to hurt Capezzi—but fast.

The next idea was to order all kinds of shit in Capezzi's name from dildos to clothes to furniture, but Frankenstein found out that this was a problem, too.

"Most mail order today," a woman from a company they called explained, "is not COD. You can order it with a Visa or Mastercard, but not COD."

It was Stein who had the idea.

"We'll go to Philly," Stein said, "call a lot of people from the Philly Yellow Pages. Make believe we're Capezzi."

"And do what?"

"I don't know. Maybe hire a guy to rip out the fence around his house. Or lay sod. Or redo the roof, or pump a cesspool. Like that."

Piccolo cackled.

"I love it. Maybe we could get someone to move the house."

Stein tittered.

"You got the idea," he said.

Frankenstein switched some tours with other detectives so they could head to Philly after an eight-to-four. They were in the city by nine o'clock. By ten they were in a room on the South Side poring over the Philly Yellow Pages. It had a lot of good stuff in it.

As they examined the book, Frankenstein decided that the ideal thing would be to get people to perform services without Capezzi's knowledge, then present him with the bill. But such notions were unrealistic; no contractor was going to do anything without first meeting with a person.

Gradually they hit upon something: call people who provided *emergency* services only. They might end up not doing anything, but just having them show up would bust Capezzi's balls.

Frankenstein figured that Capezzi's balls were so red and swollen from being squeezed that any little thing would be more than okay.

They finished going over the Yellow Pages, lining up the people to call, at one o'clock in the morning. And then Piccolo produced a surprise.

From an overnight bag he had brought with him, he produced two bottles: a small bottle of San Pelligrino for Howie and a medium-sized, empty pickle jar of guinea red for himself.

They stood opposite each other and toasted the success of their mission.

"Here's to Angelo Capezzi," Piccolo said, "may his balls roast in hell. And let the Ferret look down from heaven and shower that motherfucker with balls of shit."

"Frank," Howie said, "you have a gift with words."

And then commenced the mental ward laughing tape.

Chapter 33

Lawless checked the number of Dr. Bloom's answering service in the Cowles reverse directory, where you can get addresses from phone numbers, and found that the company listed for the number belonged to L and L Telanswerphone, its address was on 178th Street and Hillside Avenue in the Forest Hills section of Queens, and it was in the 106.

Forest Hills was still a beautiful area of the city, with particularly good-looking apartment buildings, but there were also many lovely private homes made of red brick with orange-tiled roofs. Most of them were set on well-maintained lawns.

Hillside Avenue ran through Forest Hills, a main drag flanked on both sides with all kinds of stores, some quite ugly, supermarkets giving no hint of the quiet residential blocks behind them.

L and L was located on the second floor of a two-story brick building above The Greenery, a florist shop.

Lawless climbed a long flight of stairs that terminated in a heavily reinforced door. He rang a bell, and a few seconds later someone looked through a peephole.

"Yes?"

Lawless showed his shield.

The door opened. A heavyset black woman with a worrisome look let him in.

"What's the matter?" she asked.

"Nothing. I'd like to speak with the manager."

"Oh. Please come with me."

Lawless followed the woman down a short hall.

They passed an open doorway to the left, and he glanced in. Three operators, all wearing phone headgear, were sitting in front of computers.

The woman led him through another open doorway on his right.

It was a small office with a single desk. There were some framed letters on the walls. A fashionably dressed, thin black woman sat behind the desk, which was very neat.

"Lil, this is a policeman. He wants to talk to you."

"Yes?" she said.

She stood up, a worried look on her face.

"You have a client," Lawless said, "a Dr. Bloom . . ."

She shook her head.

"Did have. He canceled."

"When was this? We called today."

"He pays a week ahead. The service is terminated at the end of the week."

"So he's still getting messages and could call in for them."

"Right. But he never got many messages."

"Who called him?"

"One man called him, and a woman. A couple of other people here or there. I wondered why he needed the service at all."

"When did he cancel?" Lawless asked.

She sat down and typed something on a computer. She waited while some information came up, then turned.

"November tenth," she said.

"How long did he have it?"

She glanced at the screen again.

"Since June first."

"Do you have his address?"

"He never gave it. He said that he was a psychologist and didn't want people bothering him at his home."

"How about his number?"

"Don't have that, either."

"How did he pay?"

"Money order. I'd get a money order on the first of the month."

"Did you ever meet him?"

She shook her head.

"Everything was done by mail."

"Never gave any hint of where he might live?"

"No."

They sat in silence for a while.

"What's this all about, anyway?" Lil said.

"Just some routine stuff," Lawless said, "but it may be criminal. I would appreciate it if you don't tell him we've been making inquiries if he should call in."

"No problem."

Lawless paused a moment. Then:

"Do you have records of those money order payments?"

"Sure. We have 'em all. Keeps people friendly in case of a dispute."

She went into a file drawer and came up with the receipts quickly and handed them to Lawless. He thanked her and left.

Lawless called Racanelli from the street, but he wasn't there. He left word for him to call him at the station.

He was going to tell Racanelli that Dr. Bloom was acting like a man who was covering his tracks.

And who seemed to be a man who had a special purpose for setting up an answering service that had little, if anything, to do with business.

But what really bothered Lawless was the date Dr. Bloom canceled his service. It happened to be the day after Spano died—or was murdered.

CHAPTER 34

Frankenstein started making the calls at nine o'clock the next morning. Since there was only one phone in the room, and to save time, they divided the numbers they were going to call in half. One of them would use the hotel phone, and one a street phone nearby. It all had to be done at high speed.

The fates seemed to be on their side. Though November, the temperature was in the mid-fifties and the sun was out. Whoever used the booth wouldn't get cold.

As they had discovered the night before, there were hundreds of companies who provided emergency services of various kinds. There were companies who would clear your drains, unplug your chimney, handle a pest problem, pump a cesspool, board up a house, plug a leak, open a door, fix a furnace.

There were lawyers, dentists, and doctors, who would come to your house.

But they decided on contractors. Contractors promised to be the most disruptive.

At first, Frankenstein was going to try to arrange the visits of the contractors so they would all arrive at the same time. But it was too difficult to keep track. They figured if they called enough people, more than a few would arrive at the same time. They just told everyone they called to show up "*as fast as possible—please*."

As they made the calls, an interesting phenomena took place: both men started to believe they really had the problems they were calling about. After a while, their performances were definitely Oscar material.

* * *

For the third straight night, McKenna had parked on the road maybe seventy-five yards from the pier closest to where Capezzi's boat had been.

It seemed even more desolate than Penrose Street, and certainly it was colder. The night wind came off the river and found its way into the car. Every now and then he would run the car to get warm.

He had been there for three days, and during that time he had seen relatively few cars. Most of these were filled with people who had been parked near the bar.

After ten, when the bar closed, the traffic was virtually nonexistent.

Tomorrow, he thought, it would be a week since the boat was sunk.

On each of the last two days he had received calls from Capezzi wanting to know of his progress. He had never seen the wop so anxious.

McKenna watched. He hoped he would get a break soon.

CHAPTER 35

By ten o'clock, Frankenstein checked out of the motel and drove to Penrose Street.

Between them, they had gotten promises from sixty-two contractors of various kinds, including fifteen firms who pumped cesspools, to come as quickly as possible.

"I like the irony," Stein had said to Piccolo on their way to the street.

Piccolo liked it, too.

By ten-twenty, Frankenstein pulled into Penrose Street.

They parked about seventy-five yards from Tiny's and had an unhampered view of the place.

An exciting, wonderful sight greeted them.

There were two big trucks parked near the shack; both looked like sanitation trucks. And another big truck, belching exhaust through twin stacks, had just turned into the block and seemed to be slowing down.

There was also a panel truck parked in front. It was red—a little red ballbreaker.

Outside the shack, it looked as if one of Capezzi's goons—a big, beefy guy with black hair—seemed to be arguing with one of the drivers, who was in the cab of the truck.

Frankenstein could hear their voices getting a little loud, then exhaust spewed from the twin exhaust pipes, the truck growled, and the driver started to drive away, sticking his hand out the window, middle finger raised.

A moment later, a uniformed guy emerged from the shack and went to the red panel truck. As it went by them, Frankenstein got a glimpse of the driver's face—he looked very pissed—and could read the small sign on the side of the door, which they hadn't been able to read before: FRANK'S RADIO PLUMBING.

The other truck that had turned into the block stopped by the shack while the driver of the other truck was exiting the shack. The goon was waving the other truck away, but the driver, apparently confused, came to a stop anyway.

The goon made it clear.

"Get the fuck out of here!" he yelled.

There was a brief hesitation, then the big truck lumbered away, followed shortly by the other truck. There were no more vehicles outside the shack, and the goon went back inside.

Frankenstein waited. They said nothing, but the air was alive with their hope.

For the next five minutes, the few vehicles that came down the block passed the trailer.

Then, coming from behind them, Piccolo heard the growling roar of a very big diesel engine. He glanced in the side-view mirror and saw a truck with a tubelike red top coming toward him.

"Please," he said, and Howie swiveled his head to get a better look.

The truck went by, starting to slow up, maybe looking for an address.

Printed in letters that were formed from drawings of playing cards was the legend:

A ROYAL FLUSH BEATS A FULL HOUSE

"Thank you, God!" Piccolo whooped.

"*Mazel Tov,*" said Stein intensely.

The truck stopped right in front of the shack. A goon virtually exploded from it, and Frankenstein could see him gesticulating at the driver, the word *fuck* being used as noun, verb, and adjective in his sentences.

The truck started up and was moving away when the driver got his revenge: he let loose with a long blast of his air horn, which seemed to shred the sky, made gooseflesh bloom on the backs of Frankenstein's arms, and made the goon's hands spring to cover his ears as he disappeared into the shack.

Frankenstein cackled and tittered and suppressed roaring.

Simultaneously, two more vans stopped in front of Tiny's, both in panel trucks. One said: MR. CHIMNEY MAGIC, and the other ASSURED LOCKSMITH. The men, one in a blue uniform, the other in green, chatted briefly with each other, then went inside.

While they were inside, another van went by Frankenstein, this one for handling emergency pest control. They had called a number of pest control companies.

A minute later, the men were on their way back to their vans. The goon had followed them out.

A few minutes later, another small green panel truck appeared.

It was a Roto-Rooter truck.

Then, from the other way, came another small panel truck. It was a battered powder blue job, and Stein could make out part of the logo on the side: a paint brush with paint dripping off it . . .

"Good. The cesspool guy can pump the shit out, and this guy can paint it," Piccolo said.

As they spoke, a couple of more men came out of the shack. They had black hair and wore suits and were large.

Soon, the Roto-Rooter truck had driven away, but the painting truck had parked. The goons were waving him off.

At ten forty-five, Frankenstein left their perch and drove to a phone on the street two blocks away. Piccolo made the calls.

Then they drove back to their spot to observe. If Domino's fulfilled their advertising claims, Capezzi should be receiving a dozen pizzas from three different Domino's within the next ten minutes.

They did. Seven minutes after the first call was made, a battered old Ford wheeled up to the shack, made a screeching halt, and a young guy got out bearing a stack of pizza boxes.

He went right into the shack.

"I fucking love it," Piccolo said. "Bon apetfuckingteat!"

Seconds later, the kid was exiting the shack at high speed, two goons screaming at him. The pizzas spilled out of the boxes, but the kid paid no attention and was soon gone.

Two minutes later another Domino's car appeared, and then a third. They were quickly driven away by goons.

For the next half hour, the stream of trucks continued.

But there was, as it were, a centerpiece of Frankenstein's presentation to Capezzi. And just about eleven-thirty, and at the perfect moment—there were three panel trucks, a cesspool truck, and a small crane truck parked outside the shack—a big, odd-looking white truck drove into view.

"Jesus Christ," Piccolo said. "Hallelujah!"

It was the mobile truck of WSBK, one of the three TV stations Frankenstein had called.

The truck's occupants sprang into action like demented roaches.

A young woman with bobbing red hair, wearing a purple suit, was on the street in fifteen seconds; directly behind her was a cameraman with a minicam.

Instantly the three goons who were shouting at the contractors tried to soften their approach, but the red-haired roach was having none of it. She stuck a microphone toward one of them as he talked, and he turned angrily and walked away.

The other two stayed, raising their voices.

Then the lady did her Cecil B. deMille, shooting the trucks and the drivers. Then she started to talk to them . . . while another couple of trucks pulled up, parking opposite Capezzi's place and now completely blocking off the street.

"I got a great idea," Piccolo said, "a 213."

"Fantastic," Howie said, "brilliant!"

A moment later they had backed the car up, hung a U, and were down the block. They screeched to a stop at the phone they had used to call Domino's.

Piccolo tapped out the number.

Three rings later a 911 operator came on.

"Oh, God," Piccolo whined, "oh, God. There are a bunch of guys beating a police officer up real bad . . . Oh . . ."

"Where?" The voice, which had been low key, suddenly was sharp and edgy.

Piccolo gave Tiny's address.

They had barely gotten back to their catbird seat to view the proceedings when they heard the first siren, proving once again that if you wanted a cop fast, just tell him another cop's in trouble.

Within two minutes, three Philly blue-and-whites, lights flashing, sirens screaming, screeched into the block and, moments later, cops poured out, a couple of guns drawn.

The street was absolutely gridlocked, and one of the drivers started to blast his air horn. It was a madhouse.

Then Piccolo started to sing:

"Sugar in the morning, sugar in the evening . . . ain't we got fun."

And Howie joined him. It was Bellevue time in the Trans Am, Bellevue time on the street.

In a word, perfect.

The circus at Tiny's lasted more than an hour, and Frankenstein stayed and watched the whole thing. Eventually the other two TV stations they had called showed up, and a small crowd had gathered.

All told, Frankenstein figured about two-thirds of the contractors they called showed, including all six Domino's pizzas and enough cesspool trucks to keep Veterans Stadium shit free.

Unhappily, Jabba did not emerge, though Frankenstein was pretty sure he was in the shack. But it was nice thinking of him in there, his balls roasting, chaos around him, disrespect showering down on his ugly wop head.

They left after the second hour, but stopped at the corner to make one call. To the shack.

It rang, and a goon answered.

"Yes," Stein said, Piccolo listening, "is Mr. Capezzi there. This is Captain Jacobs of the Fifth Precinct."

"Just a minute."

"Yes." It was Capezzi. It was going to be a perfect ending to a perfect day.

"Listen," Piccolo said, "this is one of the men who runs scrotum pullers anonymous. We were wondering if you ordered a pizza."

The next thing Frankenstein heard was a dialtone.

How sweet it was!

Chapter 36

The week following his visit to the L and L answering service was a particularly busy one for Joe Lawless and the squad, which was not unusual granted the time of year. It was close to Thanksgiving, and Christmas wasn't too far away. Homicide and suicide—particularly suicide—became more popular around holiday time.

Actually Lawless didn't particularly mind the delay in working the Werner case, because he had noticed something significant about the half dozen money order receipts the answering service owner had given him.

All had been purchased at the same store, and all had been purchased on a Sunday, every seven days. As it happened, Sunday was the first day he could get back to the case. Maybe somebody who worked Sundays would remember who bought them.

He had traced the money orders to a 7-Eleven in the Bay Ridge section of Brooklyn. It was another area—probably the only one in Brooklyn—that had wise guys protecting it. Which meant it was clean, the buildings—primarily five-story brick—well maintained, the streets safe to walk.

The 7-Eleven was on Vermeer Street and was operated by Indians.

He entered the store around noon on Sunday.

There were two guys dressed in white shirts behind the counter and a young dark-skinned woman with a red dot in the middle of her forehead.

Lawless stood back while a couple of customers were waited on by one of the men, then stepped up. He flashed his shield, smiled.

"How are you doing? My name is Lawless. I wonder if you have a couple of minutes to speak with me?"

"What you want?"

"A couple of minutes."

He stared at Lawless for a moment, then muttered something to the woman, and came around the corner.

Lawless reached into the breast pocket of his jacket, withdrew the money order receipts, and handed them to the man.

"If you look at them," Lawless said, "you'll notice that all were bought here, for the same amount, and every Sunday."

Slowly the man looked at them, then leafed through a couple.

"What I need to know," Lawless said, "is who bought them."

The man glanced up from the receipts.

"I don't know," he said, smiling slightly.

"I don't need a name. Just a description."

The man shook his head.

"How about your workers?"

The man's eyes flashed with annoyance, but he said nothing. He handed the money orders back to Lawless and walked away.

Lawless waited until the Indian woman was finished waiting on an old lady, then walked over and explained what he wanted.

"I usually don't work Sundays," she said. "I'm just filling in for my brother. He went to Delhi yesterday." There was only the slightest trace of an accent.

The woman looked at the money order receipts.

"Sorry," she said, "can't help."

Lawless nodded, then turned to his right, and looked. There was a kid there loading beer into cold cases.

"Does he work here on Sundays?" Lawless asked the woman.

She nodded.

Lawless took the receipts from her and walked to the back of the store. The kid was putting in six-packs.

"How you doing?" Lawless said.

The kid turned around and looked up.

"I was wondering if you could help me. I'm a detective with the fifty-third precinct, and I'm trying to find someone who bought some money orders here."

The kid stood up. He was tall, pimply faced. He was a little nervous. Probably had a toke in him. Most kids today did.

Lawless explained further.

"You work behind the counter on Sundays, right?"

"Yeah, either that or I'm doing stuff in the back."

Lawless handed the money orders to the kid.

"They're all bought on Sunday for the same amount. Remember who bought them?"

The kid leafed through them.

When he came to the last one, he paused.

Then he shook his head.

"I thought I remembered a guy . . . I'm sorry, I can't help."

"This guy might have been driving a flashy red car," Lawless said.

Lights came on in the kid's eyes.

"Fire-engine red?"

"Yes."

''Okay! A Corvette, red corvette, about a 1984 model. Old with all the glass in back. Yeah, I remember the guy. I saw him park outside a few times.''

''What'd he look like?''

''Short blond hair . . . a little missing . . .''

''How old was he?''

''Old. As old as you.''

The kid's face reddened; he realized he'd said something insulting.

Lawless disregarded it.

''Forties?''

''Yeah. He was in his forties, I think. I remember asking him about the car, but he wasn't very friendly. Yeah, he was the dude who bought the money orders every Sunday.''

''Good. Anything else you can remember?''

''No. Just the car. It was in mint condition.''

''Let me take your name and number in case I have to call you again.''

''My name's John Gruetzke . . . I ain't going to get in trouble, am I?''

''No way. I'll also give you my card,'' Lawless said, taking out a card and handing it to the kid. ''If he comes in again, don't say anything to him, but try to get the plate number. Okay?''

''Oh, sure,'' the kid said. ''I'll do that. What'd this guy do?''

''Maybe nothing,'' Lawless said. ''We just want to talk to him.''

''Oh.''

CHAPTER 37

Lawless called Racanelli from a phone outside the 7-Eleven. He wasn't in, so Lawless left a message for him to call back.

The kid had given him a very good lead. There couldn't be that many 1984 red Corvettes around. And, hopefully, the guy lived in the neighborhood where he bought the money orders.

That was the best scenario. But if this guy was a perp, he'd be careful; it might not go down that easily.

Lawless called a guy named Holmes who worked in Central Communications. Holmes said that he would put the car in the system in the Bay Ridge area and see what he came up with.

Then he headed back to the squad room.

There were two calls waiting for Lawless when he got back to the squad room—one from Racanelli and the other from Holmes.

He called Holmes first.

"We've got thirty-seven registered red 1984 Corvettes in the city," he said, "and eight red ones in Brooklyn."

"And in Bay Ridge?"

"One," Holmes said, "to a Raymond Miller, Jr."

"What's his residence address?"

"It's 23-45 Bismarck, Bay Ridge."

"A doctor?"

"He's on the force."

"What? Where?"

"One oh two."

"What's he look like?"

"Let's see," Holmes said, pausing. In the background, Lawless could hear a jumble of sounds: computers, ringing, voices. . . .

Holmes came back on the line.

"He's forty-five, has blond hair, blue eyes, is five-ten."

"What about the others?" Lawless asked. "Any of them have blond hair?"

Homes gave him the descriptions of the other seven registrants. Lawless felt like a cigarette. He lit up.

A minute later, Holmes was finished. He hung up.

Racanelli, he thought, was not going to like this. Neither did he.

CHAPTER 38

Two hours later, Lawless was sitting in Ono Racanelli's office on the sixth floor of the Bronx County Courthouse. Lawless had arrived only two minutes earlier.

Lawless had just finished telling him about the guy with the red Corvette from Bay Ridge—who also happened to be a cop. Lawless told Racanelli he had done some research on Miller.

"What did you find out?" Racanelli said. His eyes had a particular quality Lawless knew only too well; he was tense, very tense. Tense and dangerous.

"He's a squad detective. General stuff. My contact says he's just an ordinary cop."

"Dirty?"

"No, not as far as Jeff knows. There *is* one thing though. . . ."

"What's that?"

"He's got a rep for being a hard guy. Has a number of brutality complaints filed against him. He was involved in an incident a year ago where a black guy he'd collared died on the way to lockup. Miller was accused of beating the guy to death, but no one could prove anything."

"How did your contact describe him?"

"Low key, keeps to himself. Nobody knows much about him. He was in 'Nam."

"Married?"

"No one knows."

Racanelli nodded.

"I checked with IAD. No complaints against him. I'm getting a copy of his file—should be here later today."

There was a silence. Then:

"I'd like to get into his house, see what's there. So far, we have no way to link him to Irmgard."

"Do you have probable cause for a warrant?" Lawless asked.

Racanelli got up, turned, looked out his window at the park.

"Maybe. A lot of it depends on the witnesses. First, I want to get the guy who saw the car near the house, see if he can ID it . . . and Miller."

"Then the 7-Eleven kid. See if he recognizes him."

"Do a lineup?"

"Not at the station. A carousel," he said, referring to the practice of letting witnesses view color slides of various people, among whom are suspects.

"I also want to see if I can get a sample of Miller's handwriting—so we can have a handwriting expert compare it to what's written on the money orders. If we can link him to Irmgard that way, I think I can get a judge to sign a warrant."

"Something's definitely going on here," Lawless said.

"No question," Racanelli said, turning away from the window.

His eyes were burning.

CHAPTER 39

On Friday, a week after the sinking of the *Maria*, McKenna was still on stakeout at the marina. A couple of times lovers had come down and parked and he had questioned them, but with no results.

Nothing had come in from his cop contacts or the snitch network.

The latest hit had made all the papers, as well as all three local TV networks. It was probably just a matter of time before one of the national networks would pick it up.

Capezzi had called him and offered an additional two large to track the humps breaking his balls. He was being driven nuts.

McKenna had turned it down.

"No, thanks, Angelo," he said. "You hired me to do a job, and I'm giving it a hundred percent. Extra money isn't going to make me work any harder."

And if he took the extra two large, then Capezzi might think that he wasn't working hard enough.

At around eleven o'clock, he took a piss in the plastic hospital bottle that was standard equipment on a stakeout. Sometimes getting laid was standard, too. More than once he and a partner, on stakeout in a van, had imported some street talent for a quick hump or blow job. It definitely broke the monotony.

But with what some broads were carrying today, a blow job could get you blown away.

He got out of the car with the bottle, walked down to the dock to stretch his legs.

He emptied the bottle in the river and was on his way back to the car, when he noticed that the lights had gone on in an apartment on the third floor of a building a short distance away.

He got back in the car.

As he waited, he would glance up at the lit apartment windows and occasionally see someone come to one of the windows and look out. Every so often he would see a couple of people pass in front of the window and the flash of lights—orange, green, blue.

A few times he observed someone entering the building. Young kids. He sensed they would be going up to the apartment.

Because it was chilly, McKenna had kept the car windows closed, but soon he let the one on the driver's side down a few inches.

The sound was instantly apparent. Low, muted, rhythmic—more a steady thud than a musical sound. The sound was coming from the apartment; they were having a party.

He waited another few minutes, then got out of the car and went over to the building. He had first removed his nine-millimeter, semiautomatic from an armpit holster and put it in the pocket of his sports jacket, where he could get to it quickly if he had to.

He went up to the front entrance of the building and looked in through the heavy, wood-framed glass doors. There was a small lobby, then beyond that two more doors with curtains on them, so he really couldn't see what was beyond.

He tried the outside door. It was open, so he stepped into the small lobby, closing the door behind him.

Then, hesitating for just a moment, he opened the inside door.

Immediately there was a sweet smell. Perfume. The last two kids who went in were girls. Maybe working girls.

A long flight of dimly lit stairs lead upstairs. He climbed them. With each step he took the music, talking and laughter got louder.

Happily it was on the second rather than the third floor.

He slipped his hand inside his coat pocket and rang the bell. Almost instantly the door swung open.

A handsome kid with a Penn State jersey on and a bottle of beer in one hand looked at him. He seemed worried. Behind the kid the place was smoky, crowded. It wasn't just any smoke. It was pot. That was good. They were illegal.

McKenna flashed the N.Y.P.D. shield, and the kid looked really concerned. Behind him, almost as if the kid had signaled, things quieted down.

"Hey, kid, I'm not here to break up your party. I just want to ask a few questions."

The kid nodded. He seemed a little relieved.

"What's your name?"

"Rob."

"Okay, Rob," McKenna said, "do you have parties like this every week?"

"Yeah, more or less."

"Have one last Friday?"

"Yeah."

"Okay, what I'd like to know, Rob, is if anyone saw anybody messing with any of the boats."

McKenna could tell the kid knew what he was talking about right away. The kid smiled a little, but tried to hide it.

"Yeah, we heard about the sinking. Uh-huh."

"Anybody see anything?"

"I don't know. I think one of the girls who was coming in saw someone down by the pier."

"Can I speak to her, Rob?"

"I guess. Can you wait a minute?"

McKenna nodded.

The kid closed the door, and ten seconds later it opened again. Standing there was a little dark-haired girl who was probably younger than McKenna's youngest daughter. She had nice tits.

"My name's Jenny. May I help?"

"Last week Rob said that you may have seen something related to the sinking of the boat."

"I don't know," the girl said. "All I saw were two guys."

"Can you give me some more details?"

"I was on my way into the building and I saw two guys walking down the pier toward the water. I thought it was odd; it was so late and all."

"You didn't see their faces?"

She shook her head.

"No. I just saw them from behind."

"Anything unusual."

"They were odd-looking. One guy was very big, and the other very small. In fact, at first I thought it was a kid, but then I noticed he walked like a man."

"That's it, huh?"

"Yes. I didn't think anything of it. But then when I heard about the boat . . . I thought maybe they had something to do with it."

McKenna nodded.

"Yeah, okay. Thanks for your help, Jenny. You can go back to your party now."

"Thanks."

As she turned and walked away, McKenna noted that she had a nice ass, too.

McKenna stayed on stakeout until four A.M. The party was still going when he started his drive back toward the motel he called home.

From time to time he would think that whoever those guys were, they had to be the ones who sank the boat. But all he had was a big guy and one little guy. A Mutt and a Jeff.

Vaguely there seemed to be a connection between the description of the two guys and something in his mind. . . .

Then he started to remember. Last year, when he was checking the snitch out for Capezzi, he had tracked a photo taken of a big guy delivering a clipped Caddy to Philly.

He had learned that he was a detective on the job for the N.Y.P.D. And that he had a partner. A little guy.

The big guy was a Yid named Stein, and his partner was a little wop, Piccolo.

He remembered more.

He had found out that they were trying to sting Capezzi, and that it had all started because a truck had been stolen from the little wop's nephew.

And the snitch had helped them get inside.

Telling Capezzi about the Ferret had been worth a good payday.

McKenna wondered.

Could it be? They had the physical pedigree, but why would they be breaking Capezzi's balls. Over a snitch? Didn't make sense to go to such lengths.

McKenna remembered looking at the Jew—Stein's—personnel jacket. He seemed to have a few screws loose.

Maybe—just maybe—they were behind all this.

McKenna fired up the car. He would look into it. But he would not say anything to Capezzi unless it worked out. He didn't want to raise that wop's hopes too high.

CHAPTER 40

It was eight at night and Frankenstein was near the end of their tour, which had started at eight in the morning.

They were in the squad room, Stein typing up their DD5s.

They had investigated a heist, an OD, and a killing—one Dominican drug dealer by another.

On the way home, they stopped at the Blue Moon Diner for dinner, as much to eat as to hopefully have a stickup team come in.

Frankenstein's plan was simple: shoot them.

"That will probably stop them," Piccolo said.

Stein ate only healthy foods, like salads and vegetable dishes—he was practically a vegetarian—while Piccolo favored death dealers—bacon, pork, eggs, and all the other no-nos doctors counseled against.

His philosophy was simple: he figured that at any given moment he could get killed, so he wasn't going to worry about heart disease in ten years.

They finished their meal at about nine o'clock, paid the full tab—they figured the Onassis brothers didn't need cops eating on the arm—and left.

They stood outside the diner for a moment, Piccolo smoking. As they did, their eyes scanned the burned-out scene for action, something they did as naturally as breathing. There didn't seem to be any.

"So what do you want to do?" Stein asked.

"I got to clean their cages," Piccolo said, referring to the monitor lizard, boa, python, and Tasmanian devil, "and that takes awhile."

Stein laughed.

"Sure," he said, "and you want to make sure you don't lose a hand in the process."

"Hey," Piccolo said, "they wouldn't hurt me. They love me. They also know that if they try I will kick their asses to Hoboken and back."

Stein laughed.

"What do you mean Hoboken? There are no Tasmanian devils in Hoboken."

"Okay," Piccolo said, "Newark. You wouldn't deny that, would you?"

"No way." Stein said, laughing. "Newark's got everything."

They walked down the block to Piccolo's car. It was just the way they had left it, a sleek black beauty that Piccolo loved as much as his pets. If it had belonged to someone else it would have been fair game for chop shop artists. But the street people knew it belonged to Piccolo.

Piccolo started the car and eased it out onto the street.

Ten minutes later, he was pulling onto 205th Street and Mosholu Parkway. He rented a garage there. Never knew when somebody would happen by who didn't know who the car belonged to. Or kids. Today's real young kids didn't give a shit about anything.

They started to walk from the garage to the building where they lived.

"Look at those trees," Stein said. "What a shame!"

He was referring, more accurately, to the stumps of trees along Mosholu Parkway that had recently been cut down to make way for an apartment complex.

"Yeah," Piccolo said, "now the brothers got no place to live."

McKenna, in his Cadillac, was not close enough to see the pained expression on Stein's face. But he was close enough to have followed them to the site, watching as they parked the car.

But McKenna was a little tense. These were not civilians. These were cops. Most cops were suspicious, ever alert to a tail.

And these were not ordinary cops. You work in Siberia a while and you are either street smart or you are gone. These had to be very street smart cops.

McKenna didn't like it. If he took a burn, things could get fucked up. He wanted to deliver them to Capezzi, but in a nice neat package. He would have to approach the problem another way.

CHAPTER 41

In any trial, it is a truism that the judge overseeing it is super important.

Jorge Vasquez, a crack dealer in Manhattan, shot another dealer to death and copped a plea before Judge Donald Blake, who had a reputation for being liberal. Vasquez got five years for the murder.

Evangelist Jim Bakker robbed his followers of money and received forty-five-years-to-life.

More than sentencing, though, the judge can change the way a trial is conducted by his attitude as it goes along. Consciously or unconsciously, it can keep an attorney from objecting when he should, or hurt his concentration, or dilute the verve with which he approaches the case.

Judges make a big difference.

Nobody understood that more than Ono Racanelli. In his mind he had a list of preferred jurists, and if the case were important enough, he would do whatever he could to get the judge he wanted.

In this case, Ira Skolnick was to preside at the trial, and Racanelli certainly had no objection. In court circles Skolnick was jokingly referred to as Judge Roy Bean's only Jewish descendant.

Skolnick was tough, conservative, even testy. He ruled his court with an iron fist and seemed to have never heard of minimum sentences or copping a plea. If you were convicted of a crime in his court, chances were you would be doing heavy time.

Judge Skolnick showed his bent just three days after he was assigned. Without fanfare he quickly granted Racanelli a warrant to search the home of Raymond Miller.

For one thing, both the kid in the 7-Eleven and the old black guy had picked Miller out of a carousel lineup.

Both people had also identified Miller's Corvette.

Also, the handwriting expert, a guy named John Keller, had said that in his opinion the handwriting on the money orders given to L and L Answering Service was written by the same man as in the sample provided, a photocopy of a handwritten DD5 report. The report was written by Raymond Miller.

Racanelli and Lawless, armed with the warrant, first met in his office to plan it out thoroughly. Serving a warrant could always be a tricky business, but there was a growing sense that they were dealing with a very slick article in Raymond Miller. And a dangerous one.

"When do you think we should effect this, Joe?"

"The sooner the better," Lawless said. "And when we hit him, it's going to have to be hard and fast. I have my doubts that we'll find something incriminating, but I think our best shot is to hit him when his guard is down the most—maybe at night."

"We'll find out what his tours are, try to get to him after he's gone to bed—when he's most vulnerable."

Lawless nodded, then said:

"I think we should do it as undercover as possible. If he's got something incriminating in there, he may be able to get to it before we can get in."

"What do you suggest?"

"A woman. I wish Barbara could do it," he said, referring to his wife, "but she was in the papers a few years ago. Miller might recognize her."

"We can get someone else. Maybe Joan Riordan."

Joan Riordan was a petite blonde in her early thirties, but she looked eighteen or nineteen. She had often dressed up as a teenager and gone "trolling for bluefish."

"Sounds good," Lawless said.

"Okay," Racanelli said, "let's get on it."

Chapter 42

Racanelli and Lawless learned that Miller's next tour was a four-to-twelve. Theoretically that meant he should be home around one or two.

By three o'clock in the morning, the team that was to serve the warrant had assembled in Ono Racanelli's office, and by three-ten, loaded into two cars, they were on their way. Joan Riordan drove alone in a third car.

In one car was a team of five heavily armed detectives, Racanelli and Lawless were in the other.

Joan Riordan was dressed to look like a young hooker, complete with short purple satin dress and heavy makeup. She wore a long hairpiece. She also had on a fur coat and high heels.

One of the detectives was tempted to say that when she got off the job she would have a way to earn a living, but it was not the kind of thing you would say to her. She was a tough little piece of work and wouldn't take it.

Riordan headed the parade in a battered clunker of a car, a 1971 green Dodge Dart.

A half hour after the caravan started from the Bronx, they were within three blocks of Miller's house. They had passed by the house once.

Miller lived in a private home halfway down the middle of the street.

The street, a mix of apartment houses and private homes, was quiet, clean, and empty; it was very early in the morning. It had been snowing earlier, and the streets and sidewalks were covered with a thin blanket of undisturbed, powdery snow. Both sides of the street were lined with parked cars; they had not seen any Corvettes, red or otherwise.

Riordan picked up the radio from under the dashboard.

"Ono?"

Racanelli, in the car about fifteen yards behind her, picked up his mike and answered.

"Looks good. Go."

Her car started to roll down the block.

The plan was simple. She would stop the clunker in front of Miller's house, then go up and ring his bell. If he looked out a window before he opened the door, he would assume she was just a woman in trouble—or something else equally unthreatening.

When he opened the door, she would confirm that belief. As she talked, the cops and Racanelli would be moving down the block on foot. She would serve the warrant, raise her right hand, a signal, and they would engulf the place.

A minute after she had started down the block, Joan Riordan was climbing the porch stairs of Miller's house.

She was well inside her role, her eyes reflecting the concern of a bimbo who maybe smoked a little crack but was still worried.

Like Spano's house, this one also had double glass doors covered by curtains. The bell was on the right side of the doorframe. She pressed it.

After hearing nothing for thirty seconds, she pressed it again.

As she stood there, she sensed rather than saw that she was being watched. She waited.

Fifteen seconds later she heard the inside door open; someone stepped into the foyer. No indoor or outdoor lights were turned on. The house was totally dark.

The door opened.

In the dim light reflected from the street, she could tell it was Miller. The blond hair, goiterish eyes, about five-ten, with a normal build.

He was wearing a robe. His right hand was in his pocket.

"Yeah?" he said. The voice was low, cool.

"How you doin'?" Riordan said. "My name is Joan Riordan, detective third grade. Here's a warrant to search the premises."

Miller took it.

She raised her right hand. Her left hand was nestled in the left pocket of the fur coat, wrapped around a snub-nosed .38, finger on the trigger.

"What?" Miller said, sounding incredulous. "Do you know I'm on the force?"

"The district attorney will talk to you."

Racanelli and the other cops appeared just then. Miller had turned on an inside light.

"What's going on?" he asked as Racanelli entered the foyer.

"Irmgard Werner."

"Who?"

"You heard me."

"I don't know what you're talking about."

Racanelli looked at him. He was an ordinary-looking man. A little balder, a little thinner than in the photos. His brow was furrowed, his face a mask of innocence. But his eyes were another story. Racanelli saw cold lights in them; they were the eyes of a killer.

Racanelli didn't answer; he wanted to help the others with the search, which was already underway.

Miller, he noted, was on his way to the phone. He would bet anything he was going to call a lawyer. Dixon, one of the cops, stood near Miller; it was Dixon's job to watch everything Miller did.

"If he goes into the bathroom," Racanelli said, "you go with him."

The search took two hours and, as Lawless had suspected, did not produce anything useful. In fact, from the furniture and clothing and furnishings and other items in the house, Miller appeared to be what he was: a second grade detective making $39,756 a year.

Except that is, for the red Corvette they knew he owned.

"He's probably got an explanation for that, too," Racanelli said to Lawless at one point during the search.

"Believe it," Lawless said. "This guy's a cutie pie."

"You think he's dirty?"

"Yeah," Lawless said. "And I don't think he's going to have anything to say."

That was confirmed shortly thereafter, when Racanelli approached Miller, who had dressed and was sitting in the living room smoking.

"Miller," Racanelli said, "I'd like you to come down to my office and talk about this."

He took a deep drag from his cigarette. His eyes were bland.

"You can speak with my lawyer tomorrow."

"Who's that."

"Emil Cotter."

Something gripped Racanelli's stomach. Emil Cotter was an ex-attorney, a very clever and tough lawyer. He shouldn't have been surprised.

They had not found anything overt that linked Miller to Irmgard, but they took a stack of clothing, shoes, and the like with them for examination by the forensics people. All they could hope was that something would show up.

CHAPTER 43

Frankenstein was engaging in another brainstorming session, the fruit of which was designed to make Angelo Capezzi's life that much more miserable.

Frankenstein was sitting on the couch in the living room of their apartment. Piccolo's pets, each in its own cage in a corner of the room, were asleep.

Piccolo liked to occasionally take one of them out and play with it, but they all were getting a bit big for that. The boa was five feet, the monitor lizard a foot, the python was six feet, and the Tasmanian devil, though it only weighed a few pounds, was actually full grown. To take it from its cage at this point was, as Piccolo put it, to invite the "blizzard of '88, but instead of snow you'll have shit."

"I would say," Stein said, "that whatever we do, the marina, the shack, and his house are out of the picture. They'll be too heavily guarded."

"He owns real estate and other stuff. Johnson," Piccolo

said, referring to Stein's buddy at the ATF, "told us that."

"I know."

They were silent; then Piccolo spoke.

"The thing is," he said, "I want to shove it up his heinie in the limelight. Now we've got everybody's attention, including Jabba's, now's the time to pour salt on the wound. Blowing up some condo he owns in South Carolina ain't going to be jack shit."

Stein nodded. It was just what he was thinking, more or less.

Piccolo lit a cigarette. He smoked for a while. Both men were thinking.

"Maybe," Piccolo said, "we could hire a chopper, drop something on his house."

"Like what?"

"I don't know."

"Maybe," Stein said, "we could hire a plane to spray the place with DDT."

Piccolo smiled.

"You mean," he said, "like in that picture—"

"*North by Northwest*," Stein said. "That great scene where Cary Grant is standing in the middle of nowhere and then the plane comes out of nowhere and sprays him."

"Yeah," Piccolo said, "and then the plane crashes into a gas truck. All lives lost. I loved that."

Stein smiled.

"You would, Frank," he said, and both men laughed. The fact was that Stein liked it, too. The ferocity of it. He only objected to violence on a metaphysical level.

"We couldn't do that, though," Piccolo said.

"What?"

"Spray the house or drop something on it. I mean, it would mean hiring a pilot, plane, a chopper of some sort. What pilot's going to agree to do something like that? Unless you can fly? Or know someone?"

Stein shook his head.

They were silent again. And as they sat there, the Tasmanian devil awakened. Piccolo went over and dropped in a hunk of steak. The devil inhaled it.

He went back to the couch and sat down.

"I think," Stein said, "we have to approach this like warfare. I mean, there are plenty of tactics in warfare. Maybe we could use something . . ."

He stopped.

"What?" Piccolo asked.

"Indirection."

"What the fuck is that?"

"Many battles are fought that way. One commander tries to outwit the other. One way is to make someone think the attack is coming from one direction when it's coming from another."

"Oh," Piccolo said, "you mean you put up your dukes to fight a guy and then kick him in the balls."

"Exactly," Stein said.

"Hey," Piccolo said, "I like it."

"The question is what and where."

"Hmm."

They thought for less than thirty seconds. Piccolo ground his cigarette out and stood up.

"I might have the what. I know this guy who works in a rendering plant. He used to work in the morgue, and he told me once that what he smelled in the morgue can't compare to what comes out of a rendering plant."

"Really?"

"That's right. On a July day the smell of this stuff makes sewage smell like Chanel Number Five. It's a blend of fat, guts, gizzards, shit, a billion maggots that feed on it plus their shit, and the maggots that feed on maggot shit. Atrocious."

"Hmm," Stein said, "sounds promising. Could we get ahold of some of it?"

"You mean like a truckload full?"

Stein smiled.

"Yeah."

"Maybe. But once we got it, what would we do with it?"

"Indirection," Stein said. "Make him think we're attacking one place, then attack another. Just find a good place to dump it."

"Okay," Piccolo said. "Okay. Sounds good. We got the basic plan, we just got to work out the details."

"You got it," Stein said.

They were silent for a moment.

"I wonder," Piccolo finally said, his face serious, "if this stunt would drive Capezzi over the edge?"

Stein's face was flat, somber. But there was a deep twinkle in his eye.

"It certainly," he said, "won't drive him away from it."

Then they commenced to do their Bellevue laugh number.

Chapter 44

McKenna was tooling through St. Bonaventure Street in Camden.

He had thought about things long and hard, trying to figure out the implications of everything, what effect various actions would have.

If he was against a civilian, he would be okay. But these were cops. Cops who would suspect that people would be on their asses. Paranoia was a state of mind. He had to be very, very careful.

Too, he was almost a hundred percent sure these were the dudes squeezing Capezzi. He did not want to lose them.

All things considered, it was best to bring the wop up to speed, particularly since he needed his help.

Capezzi was in his usual spot in the back of the restaurant, doing his usual thing: eating. There was a huge platter of antipasto in front of him. Behind him were two boobs.

McKenna approach him, smiling.

Capezzi glanced up.

"Hi, Leo," he said through a mouthful of antipasto, "Sit down."

McKenna sat down.

"How you doing?" Capezzi said.

"Okay, Angelo. Okay."

"Want something to eat?"

"I just ate."

Capezzi nodded.

"You said," he said, just before stuffing a hunk of provolone in his mouth, "that you had something important."

"Yes," McKenna said, "I think I may have found out who it is that we're after."

The light reflected in Capezzi's small pig eyes changed.

"Who?"

McKenna explained about the girl spotting the guys at the marina, and how and why he thought they were the same cops—Piccolo and Stein—who tried to sting him last year.

"Why would they want to break my stones?"

"I'm not exactly sure," McKenna said, "except to say that both of them are two quarts low."

Then he added:

"Maybe it's a matter of honor," he said. Capezzi lowered his eyes. He understood that.

He took a long pull on his wineglass.

"So," he said, "what's the problem?"

"Like I said, I think it's these guys. I have to be very careful investigating this. They're cops. I need help."

"What do you need?"

"Cars," McKenna said, "four or five cars. I'm tracking

these guys, and if they see the same car behind them more than once they'll get suspicious."

"Whatever you need," Capezzi said.

"Good," McKenna said.

"When do you think you'll know for sure?"

"I don't know," McKenna said. He watched Capezzi.

Capezzi nodded. Aldo, standing to the left of Capezzi, suddenly piped up.

"Maybe we could get 'em in and sweat 'em."

He looked at Capezzi hopefully.

"Aldo," Capezzi said, "these are New York City cops. You don't just bring 'em in and sweat 'em. That's not too bright."

The color had gone out of Aldo's face.

"I'm sorry."

"You should be," Capezzi said.

Capezzi then stopped and looked at McKenna.

"Any idea when you might get the goods on these guys?"

"Not really. Soon, I hope."

Capezzi said nothing. He went back to eating.

CHAPTER 45

About a week after they had executed the search warrant on the home of Raymond Miller, Ono Racanelli was sitting at his desk in the Bronx County Courthouse reviewing the evidence that they had compiled.

So far, he had gathered quite a bit, including another piece just that morning: the mud sheets from the phone mounted outside the Bay Ridge 7-Eleven. The sheets showed that someone had called the Social Services facility where Spano had worked twelve times between June and November. The sheets showed that since August someone had used the phone to call the Miramar lobby phone three times.

There was no doubt in Racanelli's mind that it was Miller.

All of the evidence, of course, was circumstantial, but he also had the two witnesses that ID'd Miller.

He also intended to get a pubic hair sample from Miller; he figured by now he had enough ammunition to apply for the court order that would allow it. Hair, of course, wasn't conclusive, but it could be another piece of damaging evidence in his case—assuming there was a match.

Unfortunately the hair they recovered didn't have a root, so it was no good for DNA testing. But it could be used for something.

Racanelli stood up, stretched. He went over to the window and looked out. A light snow was falling.

Miller's attorney, Emil Cotter, was showing the kind of tenacity that made him a good lawyer. Cotter made it a habit to oppose every motion Racanelli made, even though it might be obviously irrelevant to do so. He was a fighter. His firm was a large one, with big resources, and battling him took energy.

Racanelli wondered how Miller could afford to pay him. He was certain Miller would have a logical and legal reason.

Racanelli turned from the window and sat back down at the desk.

Right now, he thought, he had enough to present this to the grand jury and could count on them to return with an indictment.

But Cotter was no ordinary lawyer, and Miller would be a devious defendant.

He opened a left-hand side drawer and took out a wrapped apple. He removed the wrapping and slowly started to eat it.

Lawless, he thought, was trying to come up with a girlfriend. So far, nothing. He had been married, but no one knew who she was.

They couldn't find Spano's wife, either. Preliminary investigation had shown that he'd been divorced for six years. He would love to talk to someone close to either man.

The phone rang. Racanelli picked up.

It was Stevenson, one of the forensic technicians.

"How are you doing?" Racanelli asked.

"Fine. We may have something."

"What's that?"

"Ted Brewer, another technician here, found a drop of what looks like blood on one of the shoes. A brown loafer. We're going to try to match it to the victim's blood, see what we come up with."

"Genetically?"

"Yes."

"How long before you know?" Racanelli asked.

"A week. This kind of testing takes a bit of time."

"Good. Please do it."

Exactly one week later, Brewer, the technician who had found the blood, got back to Racanelli.

"It's Miller's blood." he said.

"You're sure?"

Brewer had a sense of humor.

"Well," he said, "the odds are about 777 million to one in our favor."

Racanelli couldn't help smiling.

And three days later he was smiling even more: a grand jury brought back an indictment against Raymond Miller.

Chapter 46

McKenna had followed Frankenstein four times in four different vehicles provided by Capezzi—and only for a few hours at a time—but he was still nervous, even though he was sure he had not been seen.

They had not done anything incriminating, but McKenna knew that didn't mean a thing.

On two of the days he followed them to a crime scene. On another to a diner in the Bronx where they had lunch, and once at night when they hassled some dealers on a Bronx street corner.

By the looks of things, they were everything his inside man said they were. The big guy clocked a couple of the guys, and the little guy, Piccolo, kicked them. They were some piece of work. The more he saw of them, the more he sensed that they were the guys who did the number on Capezzi. They were definitely more than two quarts low.

He was continually worrying about them being cops—*street* cops. Cops who worked the streets developed a very acute sense of danger and survival; it was this instinct that had him biting his nails.

A couple of times, because of the ebb and flow of traffic, he had been forced to get pretty close. Close enough to see the backs of their heads quite clearly. Close enough for them to make him. It was an unsettling thought.

All he needed, he knew, was something that would tie them to the tricks. That was all. Maybe he could toss their apartment while they were on the job. Or maybe break into the garage where the little guy kept his Trans Am.

But both places might be wired. That's all he needed.

Whatever, McKenna figured he did not want to follow them much longer. Maybe he would take a week off and come back.

Of course, by then they probably would have done something else.

Finally McKenna figured he would follow them one more day, then lay off. He decided he'd use his other personal car, a gray Toyota, to follow them. He had not used it before.

Just as he used different cars, McKenna also followed them from different points, something he could do once he found out—with just one call—what their tours were for the week. He had simply called the squad, asked for Piccolo, was told he wasn't in and that the best time to get him was days this week, nights the next.

Twice he had followed them from the Five Three. Just sat in his car a couple of blocks away until they came out, got into their own unmarked car, and took off.

Twice he had followed them from their building.

Today he parked around the corner from their house on 204th Street. He knew this was the route that they would take to the station house. All he had to do was to pick them up when they went by. It would be safer here than parking in full view of the house as he had before, even though he'd been in a different car.

Today they were on days. He was in position by seven o'clock. The last two times he had followed them to the station, they had left the house between seven-ten and seven-fifteen.

204th Street provided good cover. It was a broad commercial block, lined with stores and pretty heavy traffic at this time of day.

He waited, idly viewing the passing scene.

* * *

Frankenstein, in an unmarked police car that was as familiar to the denizens of Siberia as any blue-and-white—but much, much more feared—turned onto 204th Street.

Just a half hour earlier, they had been called by Lawless and told that there had been a drug hit in an apartment building on Anthony and 175th; he wanted them to go right there, catch the squeal direct rather than stopping at the station house.

A drug hit was not the kind of squeal they could get a "hard-on" over—Frankenstein bet the ME hadn't been there, either—but they would do it. What the hell, it was better than seeing a live dealer early in the morning.

They passed the gray Toyota that McKenna sat in and proceeded down the block, pulling up and stopping at the red light.

Piccolo, who was driving, glanced in the rearview mirror as the gray Toyota pulled out of its parking spot and allowed another car, a black Chevy, to pass it before moving into the traffic.

The light changed, and Piccolo moved the car forward. He turned to Stein.

"What say we go down Webster today," he said, referring to Webster Avenue. "See if any of the brothers are out selling."

"Why not?" Stein said.

In a normal situation, such as now, Piccolo drove slowly—almost too slowly. In an emergency situation he would give Richard Petty a run for his money.

Now was a normal situation, so he drove slowly, traveling the circuitous route it took to get to Webster Avenue.

It was at 198th and Webster that he glanced into his rearview again.

Just behind the van that was directly behind him, he caught part of the front bumper of the gray Toyota.

It occurred to him that it was the same car he had seen pulling out into traffic on 204th Street.

He had taken six separate turns to get onto Webster. It was still with him.

Without turning his head, he said: "I'm going to stop at the bodega at 198th Street."

"Why?"

"Don't look now, but we may have company."

"Where?"

Piccolo explained.

"Okay."

A couple of minutes later, Piccolo stopped the car at the corner of 198th and Webster, facing south. He got out of the car and, without looking back, went into the corner bodega, a place called Art's.

A minute later, carrying a small brown paper bag with a couple of packs of cigarettes in it, he emerged from the store and got back into the car, again without glancing back.

But once inside the bodega, he had looked back through the front window, which was almost completely covered with paper signs.

The car had been double parked while other traffic streamed past it.

He got back into the car and started to proceed again down Webster.

"We definitely got company," Piccolo said.

"Could you see the driver?" Stein asked.

"Not that good. But I saw the fucking license plate real clear."

CHAPTER 47

It took Frankenstein only until noon to find out that the registered owner of the gray Toyota was one Leo G. McKenna, and that he lived in Manhattan on 57th Street . . . and that he had been on the job.

But it took them two days to find out his pedigree—or what he was suspected of being.

Frankenstein learned the essentials from a guy named Martin Weich, a retiree who had been a detective attached to the Manhattan DA's office for a long time.

"We knew him well," Weich said over the phone, "for being dirty. He was on the pad a long time, then he got hooked up with wise guys and shortly thereafter threw in his papers."

"Because," Stein said, "he was making money?"

"Correct," Weich said.

Frankenstein was quiet for a moment. Piccolo popped the question that was on both their minds.

"Who was he mobbed up with?"

"Couple guys. Gambinos here in the city, and Capezzi down in Philly."

There was a subtle change in the air that Weich could feel over the phone, but he let pass.

Frankenstein said nothing.

They thanked Weich, hung up, then got ready to go.

In the car, they were silent a moment, then Piccolo spoke.

"He might have been directly involved with the Ferret," he said.

"Yeah. Could have found out about us pretty easy, too, the way we found out about him."

"You got it," Piccolo said.

Unstated was the idea that McKenna was still working for Capezzi, was following them in his behalf. That was understood.

"He may have been on us before this," Stein said. "Maybe he saw us meet Mullen."

Mullen was a friend of the guy who was in the fat-rendering business. Frankenstein had seen him the day before yesterday.

"Could be," Piccolo said, "but I'm not going to sweat it. It doesn't mean nothing to him. None of anything we did means anything now.

"You're right. But it will."

Piccolo said nothing. Then:

"How do you want to play this now?" he asked.

"I think if we're careful we'll be all right. Just got to watch to make sure this guy doesn't put a wolf pack on us."

Piccolo was warmed.

"That's right," he said. "Business as usual."

Stein was silent. He knew that whatever they did they were swimming in darker waters; he also knew it would never occur to either of them to turn back.

Chapter 48

Based on what he had, Racanelli planned to go for Murder Two against Miller. Three weeks after the indictment was drawn, he learned something that pointed to a motive for the murder of Irmgard, and at the same time articulated the persona of Raymond Miller, Jr.

Routine review included checking to see if Spano or Werner had any beneficiaries on their life insurance policies.

Spano didn't have any beneficiaries—he died in testate—but Werner had one: Spano.

In September, she had taken out a $125,000 policy on her life and had named Vincent Spano as beneficiary.

A further check revealed that Werner had prepaid the entire premium for a year.

CNA, the insurance company, had paid Werner's death benefit off just two weeks earlier.

The check had cleared a week before his death. He had obviously used some of the money to pay off the IRS. The rest was missing.

Racanelli was sure he would find it—hidden somewhere by Raymond Miller.

Somehow, he theorized, Miller had gotten Irmgard to sign up for the life insurance policy with Spano as the beneficiary. He killed her, and once Spano got the life insurance proceeds, he killed him.

If he was right, Miller was indeed a cold-blooded savage, because he planned the whole thing—killing both Spano and Irmgard. And money was the motive.

But Racanelli knew he had a problem: he couldn't prove it.

Reluctantly he decided to stay with Murder Two, but at least he would present his theory of the motive.

One other thing was untheoretical: he had never wanted to convict anyone as much as Raymond Miller, Jr.

Eight weeks after the indictment was drawn, the trial of Raymond Miller, Jr. opened in one of the elegant, wood-paneled, high-ceilinged courtrooms on the second floor of the Bronx County Courthouse.

It only took three days to select a jury, and the following Monday, Racanelli made his opening statement.

It only took twenty minutes, and he mostly low keyed it emotionally. You saved the fire for the end.

He merely outlined the case, which he stated was largely circumstantial, but insisted the circumstantial evidence was very strong.

He laid it out this way:

He believed that Raymond Miller had deceived Irmgard Werner in a "cold, cruel, and callous fashion, posing as a Dr. Bloom, a suitor."

"But his real purpose was to somehow get her to take out a life insurance policy on herself, naming coconspirator Vincent Spano as beneficiary so he, Miller, could kill her—and Spano—and have all the money for himself."

As was his habit, Racanelli paced back and forth in front of the jury as he spoke, but when he made his final statement, he stopped and looked at Miller, who looked blandly back at him.

"What kind of a person," he said, "is capable of behavior like this? A savage. A savage who must be separated from the rest of society for its protection. It's that simple."

Cotter made his opening statement after Racanelli. It was brief and, Racanelli thought, effective. Cotter had a personal style that reminded Racanelli of the former mayor, Ed Koch.

"Mr. Racanelli," he finished, "is a very good lawyer, but in this case he has, somehow, lost his way. Lost his way because his evidence is smoke, and he can't put his finger on it. Other than his fantastic fairy tale about cold-blooded murder, he has no motive. I would love to see him prove the connection between my client and the deceased."

"My case," he said, "will be simple. Mr. Racanelli and myself shouldn't have to keep you here too long. I will rebut the alleged witnesses Mr. Racanelli has, and I will introduce doubt, reasonable doubt, I think, about his physical evidence. Thank you.''

Racanelli first called the ME, Vic Onairuts, and a series of forensic technicians who testified on the various physical aspects of the case.

He also called the technicians and detectives who worked the scene, including Joe Lawless.

Cotter was quiet during this portion of the testimony, engaging in very little cross-examination of the witnesses. That was not a surprise. None of the testimony directly tied Miller to the crime in any way.

The scenario was considerably different when Racanelli called Otis Blake, the old black guy who said he spotted Miller with Irmgard outside the DeLuxe Theatre.

There was, perhaps, a fine line between coaching a witness and preparing him to testify, and Racanelli had spent a good four hours with Blake trying not so much to tailor his testimony—he would not do that—but to make sure he knew what to expect from Cotter.

As it happened, Cotter surprised them both.

Cotter took Blake through his direct testimony again, but then stopped at one point and said:

''Just how far were you from the man you have identified as Raymond Miller?''

''No more than twenty feet,'' Blake said.

''I see,'' Cotter said.

''Let me ask you this, Mr. Blake,'' Cotter said. ''Have you ever played baseball?''

Racanelli objected.

''Where is this going, Your Honor?'' he said.

''Yes, Mr. Cotter,'' Judge Skolnick said, ''where is this going?''

''May I have a couple of minutes? I'll demonstrate where I'm going shortly. I'd rather not say right now.''

''All right, I'll allow it.''

Cotter turned his attention back to Blake.

"Did you, sir, play baseball?"

"No, I didn't," Blake said. He looked nervous. his was not something Racanelli had covered.

"Did you play football?"

"Yes."

"Good," Cotter said.

With that, he turned and walked away from the witness stand, then down an aisle between rows of spectators and all the way back to a massive wooden entry door. He turned.

"How far is this, sir?" Cotter said.

Racanelli was on his feet.

"Your Honor," he said, "I can see where this is going. He means to impugn the witnesses's ability to make an identification by attacking the distance he thinks he was from Miller. But the witness isn't supposed to be an expert of distance."

"Sustained."

Cotter walked forward.

"All right, Mr. Blake," he said, "why don't you tell me to stop when I'm about the distance you say you were from my client when you saw him."

Everyone watched as he walked slowly forward.

" 'Bout there," Blake said.

Cotter nodded.

"This, sir, is around thirty feet—not the twenty feet you estimated."

Racanelli was on his feet again.

"We covered that issue," he said.

The judge cautioned Cotter to get off it.

Cotter turned and smiled.

"No problem," he said. "No problem."

Then he turned toward Blake.

"Let's forget the mistaken distance," he said, thereby reminding the jury of it again, "and let me ask you this."

Blake looked at him. He was clearly scared. Racanelli watched.

"You saw Mr. Miller from this distance, and you said he had blond hair and blue eyes. That's your testimony, correct?"

"Yes."

"Let me ask you this, then," Cotter said. "What color are my eyes?"

Racanelli was on his feet in a flash, but before he could object, the judge said:

"I'll permit him to answer."

Blake said nothing. Then:

"Blue," he said.

"They're brown, Mr. Blake," Cotter said. He looked at the jury, his face quizzical and sad, then back at Blake. "No further questions."

Racanelli got up for redirect and tried to salvage the witness, saying that it was a "sunny day, visibility was better. . . ."

Cotter said nothing. He knew that he had destroyed the witness.

CHAPTER 49

One gift that Racanelli had as a trial lawyer was not to grouse or simmer about bad turns in a trial. He didn't want to have one defeat affect the way he presented the rest of the witnesses and evidence.

Racanelli figured that he'd better start the next day's direct positively, so he brought out a representative from

NYNEX to testify as to the authenticity of the various mud sheets showing that Spano had called "Dr. Bloom," that Irmgard had called him from the Hotel Miramar.

He did not bring in the mud sheets showing that someone had called Spano and the Hotel Miramar from a 7-Eleven pay phone. He had not yet established that Miller had easy access to the pay phone outside the 7-Eleven. He would have to do that later. He had hired a graphologist named Lester James. James had impeccable credentials, having testified for various arms of the Department of Justice, including the FBI. Racanelli felt that juries were skeptical about people like graphologists, so the heavier the credentials the better.

Racanelli called the 7-Eleven kid to the stand about ten-thirty.

He brought him through his direct testimony in a deliberate manner, and the kid did very well, answering his questions in a straightforward manner.

After fifteen minutes, Racanelli said, "Your witness," and sat down.

Cotter was his usual smiling, charming self, but Racanelli knew he was just waiting for an opening to pounce on the kid.

"So," Cotter said, "you saw Mr. Miller get out of a red Corvette every Sunday."

"Not every Sunday. I mean, for a while—when he first came into the store—I didn't even know he owned a Corvette. But later, when I found out, I used to sort of wait for him so I could see the car."

"So you saw this red Corvette every Sunday from then on.

"Just about. One Sunday I wasn't there."

"Are you an expert on Corvettes?"

"Are you kidding? No way. I just like 'em."

"But you're sure that that red car you saw every Sunday was the same Corvette?"

"Yeah. There's no mistaking wheels like that. It's hot!"

There was slight ripple of laughter in the court; even a few jury members laughed.

Racanelli was secretly pleased. Cotter had made a mistake. In a couple of statements the witness had established his veracity and reliability.

Cotter was not about to make another mistake. A few minutes later he finished his cross and gave him back to Racanelli for any redirect. There wasn't any.

Racanelli called the handwriting expert next, and when it was Cotter's turn to cross-exam, it was clear he had done his homework.

The expert had come equipped with charts and blowups of slides, and Cotter, armed with his own pointer, debated the findings that Miller had, indeed, been the person who had bought and signed the money orders.

The handwriting expert's testimony took the rest of the morning and about half the afternoon, and when it was over, although he had not savaged it, Cotter *had* managed to dent it a bit; Racanelli was sure that Cotter would present his own handwriting expert to dilute it even more.

Still, Racanelli felt that he had built a strong circumstantial case, and the centerpiece of it—the DNA finding on the blood found on Miller's shoe—appeared irrefutable.

Racanelli had a few more witnesses to present, then he would bring in his DNA evidence.

Yes, all in all, the trial was going all right, though he never took anything for granted.

Racanelli was in his office at about nine that night when the phone rang. It was Joe Lawless.

"I found Miller's wife," he said.

"Good work."

"She lives in Chicago. Never remarried. Uses her maiden name, Lutwiniak."

"Terrific."

"How should we handle it?"

Racanelli thought a moment.

"Can you go out there?"

"Bledsoe won't like it."

"I can voucher it."

"Okay. I'll make arrangements."

"Thanks, Joe. Nice work."

They hung up.

Racanelli had not asked Lawless how he had located Norma Miller, nee Lutwiniak. And so quickly. Lawless had his ways—and some times Racanelli didn't want to know what they were.

He knew that if Lawless had to testify as to how he had gotten his information, he would have used a legal path that would stand up under court scrutiny.

Racanelli smiled.

As Lawless had said: He only used UL-rated cattle prods.

Chapter 50

Frankenstein was in their apartment in their favorite spot: Stein sitting on one side of the kitchen table sipping San Pellegrino and Piccolo on the other side, gulping guinea red.

It was sunny in the room, but there was something else there, too. Something unsaid that needed to be said.

There was a long period of quiet, and Piccolo took out a cigarette. He lit up. The smoke tumbled in the sun.

To Stein, it was a signal. A signal that there was some serious stuff to discuss. Stein broke the ice.

"Frank," he said, "I was thinking about this guy following us."

Piccolo nodded.

"And I was thinking," Stein said, "that since we don't know how long this guy was following us, we can't be sure if he saw us visit your friend Mullen out at B. A. Tofte, the rendering plant."

Piccolo nodded, but said nothing. He knew Howie had not come to his point yet.

"So," Stein continued, "if we do this thing to Capezzi, and McKenna actually followed us out to the plant, he's going to know right away it was us."

"I guess so," Piccolo said. He took a long sip of the wine.

There was a silence.

"I think you know that, right, Frank?"

"Sure, Howie."

"You know more, too, don't you, Frank?"

The slightest smile played around Piccolo's lips.

"Like what?"

"Like the whole thing had a grand design, purpose. I mean the dump job on Capezzi's trailer, the sinking of his yacht, the sting with the contractors . . . and this. You knew that Capezzi would come after you. You knew that. You knew that ultimately it would be one-on-one, *mano a mano,* with Capezzi. You didn't want to blow him away directly, you just wanted a chance to do it when he came after you."

Piccolo took a long suck on his cigarette. Smoke poured out of his nose and mouth. His face was a mixture of sadness and admiration and a slight tinge of fear.

"Howie," he said, "you're a very smart guy. You're right. I didn't know that in the beginning, but I came to realize it. Yeah, that was my real purpose."

There was a silence for a moment.

Piccolo stood up. He went over to the window and looked out, as if his eyes couldn't meet Howie's.

"The thing is, Howie, I got you into this. I mean . . . I didn't want to, but I did. And I'll tell you, Howie . . . I wouldn't want to lose you. That's all fucking mixed in there, too. In fact, I think I'd feel better if you dropped out now. I can handle those humps."

Howie shook his head.

"You know, Frank, I think you know something else you haven't said."

"What's that?"

"That I didn't just come to realize this. I've known this almost from the start. And I think you knew that when all the dust cleared, I would be there with you at the finish. And you know why?"

Piccolo turned. His eyes were misty.

"If you go," Howie said, "who's going to take care of your pets? Do you think I am going to feed a python, monitor lizard, boa constrictor, and Tasmanian devil? Hey, Frank, as you might say: 'Be fucking real.' I value my life."

Piccolo gulped and reached across the table, his hand extended.

"Hey, buddy," he said, and Stein took his hand and squeezed it.

CHAPTER 51

Piccolo was behind the wheel of the big dump truck. Stein was sitting next to him. In the back was twenty thousand pounds of raw fat and assorted abominable trimmings. The weather was cool, but they could still smell it up front. It smelled like a blend of dead meat and shit, by far the worse thing either man had ever smelled in his life. It *did* make sewage smell good.

Piccolo was smoking, something Stein welcomed.

It was half past eleven, and they were on the Jersey Turnpike, on their way to Philadelphia.

"Like old times," Piccolo said, "just like old times."

Stein laughed.

"I'll tell you," he said, "if hell has a smell, it smells like what we got in the back of this truck."

Piccolo laughed.

"Yeah, and Mullen," he said, referring to the friend of a friend who was the driver for B. A. Tofte, "says the only thing as bad as the smell is the way it looks—the maggots weigh more than the rest of the shit."

"Sounds good," Howie said, and they laughed heartily.

As much as possible, they had worked out a plan to protect Mullen in case things went wrong.

He was to stay by his phone. If he didn't hear from them by four A.M. he was to report the truck stolen. The cops might ultimately ask him why he didn't dump his load at the end of the day. He had a bullshit story all ready: he was sick, didn't feel up to it.

* * *

Frankenstein had thoroughly researched where they could unload the stuff on Capezzi's holdings, and they decided that there weren't many places.

Two days earlier, about eleven at night—so as not to be too suspicious—they drove by the trailer in a rental car.

As they suspected, the place was loaded with wise guys. There were two cars parked on the street, one on one side of the block and one on the other, and a pair of hoods in each.

It was the same story at the house. There were a couple of cars parked on the street outside, each with a pair of goons inside. Frankenstein could feel the eyes on them as they drove by.

They knew where his droppings—two of his sons—lived, but decided against trying to dump the stuff there; it just didn't feel right.

Stein's original idea was indirection; the problem was that they still had to find the right place.

Then, while driving around the block where Capezzi's house was located, they found a spot.

There was some risk involved, but they decided they weren't going to do any better.

On the other hand, if it went smoothly, it would drive Capezzi absolutely stark raving bonkers, which was the main idea.

CHAPTER 52

Timing, Frankenstein knew, was everything.

They figured that they only had maybe a minute or two to unload their precious cargo. If they couldn't do it within that time, they could be nailed. More important than anything else, they were driving a big truck. It was not exactly a getaway car.

They had to anticipate who they might be caught by. If it was the Philly cops or the like—well, maybe they could talk their way out. A quick explanation of how this was payback for a Mafia man like Capezzi whacking a good snitch, and the cops might send them on their way.

If it was the wise guys, they'd be sent on their way feetfirst. The Ferret would be getting some company.

To guard against this possibility, Frankenstein brought with them a little extra hardware to, as Piccolo said, "put the fear of the Lord in those boys."

"Yes," Howie had said as he tapped one of the pieces of hardware, "alley guns do that."

As they had gotten closer to Philadelphia, Piccolo had become more and more nervous inside. Nervous about Howie. His mind started to work up all kinds of shitty scenarios, with them all ending the same way: Howie dead.

One was really bad. Piccolo fantasized that Howie was in a grave next to Eddie Edmunton, his first partner, and Piccolo would go to visit them both.

That was a fantasy he couldn't think of for long: it really played havoc on his insides.

Howie, in this situation, was fairly calm. He just concentrated on doing the job right.

It was like when he was a kid in the school yard, and other kids—Catholic kids—would surround him and harass him because he was Jewish. They would call him a Christ killer, and would say all kinds of names that would hurt him.

He could still remember the first kid who tried to beat him up. He was a big, broad-shouldered Italian guy named Phil DePinto.

They had circled each other there in the school yard at

P.S. 46, a crowd of kids around them, and every time DePinto got a punch in, the crowd would cheer.

Howie had bided his time, waiting for a chance to throw his left, lightly poking out his right jab.

Inside he was like a furnace, with the door closed, but his face and movements gave no indication of what he was feeling.

Then DePinto, spurred on by his success, got close. He threw a right hook that missed, dropping his hand and leaving his jaw unprotected.

And Howie threw the first thunderfist of his childhood, a *whirr*ing left that caught the big kid flush on the jaw and dropped him like a sack of potatoes. He was unconscious for five minutes.

The crowd had quieted down. The kids were stunned. Howie remembered walking away, the crowd parting as he went by. He felt good, very good.

So that's the way he was now: a furnace with the door closed. When the time came, the furnace door would open, and that was it.

But Howie did worry about Piccolo, though he never explicitly told Frank that. Howie had had few friends in his life, only occasionally attracting the oddball kind of person. People, he thought, like himself.

Not that Frank was perfect.

Howie did not like many of Frank's ways.

He was bigoted against blacks and Hispanics, though not all the time. He could be nice to someone when you least expected it.

Frank didn't like Jews too much, either, except for him, but he had great admiration for their toughness, at least the Israelis.

He was a political conservative—Howie was liberal—and they were different in other ways.

But as cops, they shared the same philosophy: crush the bad guy any way you could.

And, Howie knew, the real bond was that they were alike. Misfits.

On their first reconnoiter, they had found what looked like a very good spot to wait. A place from which they could assault the beaches.

It was a parking lot behind a ball-bearing factory less than three blocks from Capezzi's house, with a phone right on the corner. Just what they needed. and they knew that once they dropped the dime, they would have to swing into action almost immediately.

It was perfect, and then fifteen minutes before they were to arrive at the parking lot, it got more perfect. It started to rain. A cold rain. Chances were that this would limit the number of goons roaming the grounds of the house.

Now they pulled onto the street where the building was located. It was shiny from the rain, with a few lights on in the row houses that lined both sides of the street; one or two blurred streetlights were glowing dimly.

And it was empty. Not a soul in sight.

Just perfect.

Then they were behind the building. Piccolo brought the big truck to a grinding halt, and Howie jumped out. He made the call. The truck was moving by the time he hung up, and Howie jumped onto the running board, then inside the cab.

Thirty seconds later, they were in the lot; both men clambered feverishly out of the cab to the back. As they did, they slipped on the gas masks that they had bought at an army-navy store. The proprietor had told them the masks could resist mustard gas.

It took them less than a minute to pull the plastic off the load of renderings.

"Christ," Piccolo said, his voice a little muffled by the mask, "I can smell this shit through the mask."

"Good," Howie said, and they both laughed muffled laughs.

Then they waited; waited what seemed like a long time, though it was only thirty seconds . . . and then they heard it: the sound of music, a distant wail, a siren.

They glanced at each other in the darkness of the cab, their eyes glittering above the masks.

Stein understood Piccolo's muffled words:

"Let's do it to it! Wahoooooooooo!"

He moved the truck through varying gears and then they were moving down the block toward Capezzi's house; or, more to the point, his property.

As the truck rolled slowly along down the street, Frankenstein kept the windows open and, indeed, there was a smell coming through, getting stronger with each revolution of the wheels.

The sound of the sirens got louder and louder and Frankenstein was almost there. The rain fell steadily, and there was still no one on the street, though they were very aware that as the sirens—another had joined the first—got louder, people who lived in the row houses might get curious.

They paused briefly at the corner, just before the block that Capezzi's property was on, waiting.

They could not see the house from the road, which was just what they wanted. They had discovered that the three acres the house was set on was rolling property, surrounded by a tall, wrought-iron, spiked fence. Just the top—the orange-tiled roof, no windows—peeked above the hill. The section where they intended to operate was blocked off by evergreens.

But they could hear, as they got closer, the sounds got closer.

Then, reflected on the low gray clouds were flashing red and yellow lights. The diversion, for whatever it was worth—and they were about to find out—was in place.

Then they glanced at each other and Piccolo moved the gears and the truck moved forward.

Just as he did, they heard another siren in the distance.

When Howie had called he had said that the fire opposite Capezzi's house was very bad. There were kids and old ladies in there, maybe trapped. It would bring the Chinese Army.

As they drove the truck into preliminary position, Frankenstein eyed the Capezzi property. There was no one there. There was no sign of life from the neat row houses either.

Piccolo came to the position he wanted. He turned the wheel, and the huge truck started to go left. He straightened it out, parts of the front wheels intersecting with the curb of the street opposite the property, then slowly backed it up.

Stein, on the sidewalk next to the fence, coaxed the truck back.

Then he was in position. Stein held up a cautionary thunderfist.

"Good," he said, "good."

Piccolo stopped.

Ten seconds later they were in position, and the sound of the sirens was loud. The timing was perfect.

Stein smiled broadly, his eyes demented, as were Piccolo's—their usual state.

"Do it to it!" Stein said.

Piccolo hit the dump elevator on the truck, and the bin lifted hydraulically. He brought it up to an angle. The back of the hopper was over the fence.

He hit the release.

A sound like spaghetti gushing from a pot ensued. Except it wasn't spaghetti. In terms of disgusting sounds it compared favorably to the sound of a power saw slowing down as an ME cut the top of someone's head off so they could get to the brain.

And it stunk—to high heaven and back.

Ten seconds later, all but fifty assorted pounds of renderings were piled up, oozing and partly alive, on Angelo Capezzi's lawn.

And Frankenstein was on their way, the hopper lowering

even as they moved, the sirens and lights totally dominating the night.

Frankenstein stopped again at the factory parking lot and, leaving the truck running, closed the hopper. At the same time, Stein was spraying the back with an industrial-strength pine oil; he just barely managed to hold his cookies intact.

Then they were on their way again.

The smell hit Capezzi's house a few minutes after the dump. Tony, one of Capezzi's button men, smelled it inside the house. He was about to go out, when Aldo came in.

"What the fuck is that?" Aldo said. "Smells like a dead animal."

"I don't fucking know," Tony said, "but it's awful."

Capezzi himself, who had been standing by the living room window watching the fire trucks, also got it.

"Find out what it is. Maybe the firemen have some chemical or something."

Except, he thought, there's not even a fire.

Tony was going to say that he'd never smelled a chemical like that, but he didn't.

When Tony went outside, he grimaced. It was really ripe. He headed down the driveway toward the gate. When he reached it, a couple of firemen came up to him.

"What's that smell?" one of them said.

"I don't fucking know," he said. "I was going to ask you."

"Not us."

"No fire?"

"False alarm," one of them said.

Tony went back into the house. Capezzi was waiting in the doorway. Tony told him it was a false alarm.

"Check out the stink. It seems to be coming from Vestry

Street,'' he said, which was on the back side of his property.

''Okay.''

Four minutes later, Tony returned, his normally tan complexion mottled. He looked like a man who had just thrown up, which, in fact, he had.

Capezzi put it all together quickly, and he was fuming when he got McKenna on a pay phone about a mile from his house. He wanted to know who was doing this—now.

It was also a case of perfect timing.

''I do know,'' McKenna said, ''for sure. About a week ago I followed these guys to a place named B. A. Tofte in Eastern Long Island—it's a fat-rendering plant.''

''Come to my house,'' Capezzi said.

''Okay,'' McKenna said, and hung up. Yes, he thought, he would love to be the beneficiary on the life insurance policy for Piccolo and Stein.

Chapter 53

Joe Lawless took an evening flight to Chicago. It was a plus-two-hour trip, but he gained an hour when the plane passed into Central time.

On another day, he would have enjoyed taking the Chicago subway into town, which you could do from O'Hare Airport, but today he didn't have time.

It had not been difficult to find out when Norma Miller would be there.

He had called her twice, finally reaching her that morning. She sounded sleepy, and he figured he had probably awakened her. She also sounded annoyed.

He told her that he was a census taker for the government and wondered when he could come by for an appointment.

"I don't know. I sleep days and work nights."

"Where do you work?"

"Barkley's, a restaurant on North Michigan, but we can't get together there. It's too busy."

"What time do you get off?"

"Midnight," she said, and then Lawless heard her voice change, she might be getting suspicious.

He quickly terminated the conversation. He told her he would speak to her in a month or so.

Lawless's flight got in at nine o'clock. On the way into O'Hare, the pilot announced that the temperature was sixteen in Chicago and a light snow was falling, but that the snow was expected to let up by the time the plane landed. That was good, Lawless thought. He didn't want to get snowed in; he had to get back to New York quickly.

He took a cab to North Michigan, a trip of about a half hour.

The snow had stopped, but there was still a slight dusting on the street, although nothing had really accumulated.

He paid the driver. The cab drove away, and Lawless stood on the street a few doors down from the restaurant, looking at it.

It seemed like a nice place. It had a glass front, neon sign; it looked well maintained.

He went inside.

It was a family restaurant. The walls on two sides were lined with booths; the center area had a number of tables in it. In the back was a small service bar.

As late as it was, the restaurant was about half filled, a tribute to how good it must be.

There were five waitresses he could see, and he immediately saw a woman who looked like Lutwiniak/-Miller. She was standing by the service bar picking up drinks. She was tall, thin, dark-haired, fine-featured. It was her.

Meanwhile, a young hostess came up and sat him at a two-seat booth near the front.

It occurred to him that he hadn't eaten all day, except for a cup of coffee and a donut at breakfast.

Lawless ordered a spaghetti dinner with sausages and a salad. He was going to pace his eating to coincide with the end of Norma's shift.

As he ate, he occasionally studied her. She had some signs of aging on her rather pretty face; wrinkles were well formed on her forehead and she had crow's feet around her eyes. He gradually formed an impression of her. She was a tense woman, worried. He didn't know if that was good or bad, or how it would figure in if he asked her to come back to New York with him.

By a quarter to eleven most of the restaurant had cleared out. He figured it was time to make his move.

The next time Norma came over to the bar, he said:

"Norma?"

She turned.

"Yes?"

"I wonder if you could talk to me a minute after you get off."

She approached him, the furrow lines on her forehead deepening.

"What about?"

"It's about your husband, Ray."

Norma's expression froze, the color drained from her face.

"Who are you?"

"Joe Lawless. I'm a cop from New York."

"Is he dead?" He detected a glint of hopefulness in her voice.

Lawless shook his head.

Wordlessly, almost sagging visibly, she picked up her drinks and transported them across the room to a young couple, one of the two last groups of people in the restaurant. Then she went past Lawless—without saying anything or looking at him—through the doorway he knew led to the kitchen.

Lawless sipped his coffee, wondering for a moment if she might have taken a powder. But that didn't matter. He knew where she lived.

But she didn't. A minute later she came out of the kitchen and went over to the young couple. She placed their bill on the table, then returned to Lawless.

"We can talk here."

She sat down opposite him.

Lawless explained the case, what had happened, how it was their theory that her ex-husband had conned and killed a woman in New York City for her insurance.

"Did you ever hear him discuss anything like that?"

"No," she said, "I didn't." And she explained that she had been separated from Miller for six months before she got her divorce—since the previous May.

Lawless tried to get her to open up about what her relationship with Miller had been like, why they had gotten a divorce.

"It was just," she said, "a clash of personalities. We just didn't get along. . . .

"Can I help in any other way?" she asked Lawless.

"If the district attorney wanted to talk to you, could you come back to New York? We'd pay expenses."

She shook her head almost violently.

"Oh, no," she said, "I couldn't leave here. I just make ends meet as it is."

"Maybe we could pay you something toward—"

"No," she interrupted, "these jobs are hard to find. I don't think so."

"I see," Lawless said. "Thanks for your help."

"Sorry I couldn't help more."

Norma called a cab for Lawless, and five minutes later he was crossing the frigid, windswept street and climbing into the back of a Yellow Cab for the ride to the airport.

At O'Hare, he checked his watch. It was eleven o'clock, Chicago time, making it midnight back in New York. Whatever.

He made the call from a bank of phones in the middle of the airport.

When Racanelli answered, he did not sound sleepy, which, in fact, he wasn't. He had been going over the scenario for the next round in court.

"How'd you make out, Joe?"

"Lousy," he said. "I talked with the wife, but she didn't really tell me anything."

He told Racanelli what Norma Miller had told him.

"I see what you mean," Racanelli said.

"What I was calling for," he said, "was to find out what you want me to do. She's lying."

"Hunch?"

"No. She told me that she left Miller six months ago. I spoke with Miller's neighbors when I was trying to find her. She's was around until just shortly after Irmgard's death."

"I see. Well, I don't think you need to do anything now. I'm in good shape as far as the trial goes. My big guns are yet to come. You can come home."

"You got it," Lawless said.

Two hours later, in the wee hours of the morning, Lawless was on an American Airlines jet as it lifted off the runway at O'Hare Airport, driving upward through a light snow.

Chapter 54

Racanelli started the day—a Thursday—following his midnight talk with Lawless, the same way he did every day: by going to mass.

He went to the same church—Our Lady Queen of Sorrows—that he had been going to since he was a little boy, and invariably to the six o'clock mass.

This did not please the two detectives, Ryan and Calabrese, assigned to keep him alive. The church itself, a huge, old, high-ceiling one, had numerous nooks and crannies where a shooter could hide himself. And it would be easy for a pro to learn that Racanelli came here every day at the same time.

Today, per usual, he went to a spot about halfway down on the right and knelt down.

The church was not crowded, there were just a few old white women and one black woman lighting candles.

In fact, Racanelli was not fixated on the possibility of dying. When he first ran for district attorney, he was very conscious of being killed, but he knew there was an unwritted law between bad guys and cops that you don't kill district attorneys. Today, of course, that had all changed.

But his death was not important, except as it related to his mother.

If he died, there would not be anyone to really care for her, and, though she was not yet infirm, one day—not too far down the road—she would be.

Still, to not pursue his career would end up making him

bitter and resentful toward his mother. That would be worse than both of them dying.

When he was in church, he felt he communicated, on some level, with God—and also with his own father.

Usually Racanelli was relaxed when he was in church, but today he was a little jumpy.

He just wondered about a couple of those old ladies in the pews. Maybe they weren't old ladies, but shooters all dressed up to be like old ladies.

And what about security, what about . . .

He realized that, yes, he was jumpy . . .

But it wasn't really about his security.

It had to do with the trial. Today was the last of the ninth, bases loaded, his cleanup man coming up. Today he would put Clifton, the DNA expert, on the stand. Clifton was the linchpin of his case and, at least on the surface, Racanelli had it made. Cotter hadn't really mounted any attack on the findings, and Racanelli knew that not everyone accepted genetic fingerprints outright. Indeed, there had been an article not long ago in *Science* magazine where a molecular biologist had attacked the DNA findings from a variety of points of view: the inaccuracy of the lab tests done, the possibility of the sample material getting contaminated, even the odds against gene matchings.

Cotter did his homework; he had to be aware of all this. So why wasn't he doing anything?

And that, Racanelli thought, was the source of his anxiety: Cotter just wasn't the do-nothing type. Which meant either he figured Miller's case was a lost cause—or he had an ace up his sleeve. If Racanelli were betting, he'd put his money on the ace.

He blessed himself and stood up.

Ryan materialized from a sacristy door to the left of the altar. Calabrese, a short Italian guy who was built like a Johnny pump, was standing in the middle of the church, eyeing everything and everybody except Racanelli.

Racanelli made it back to the car without incident, an event that did not lessen his anxiety, but did a lot to alleviate the anxiety of the cops guarding him.

CHAPTER 55

Herbert Clifton, M.D., looked like a scientist. As he strode down the middle aisle toward the witness-box, Racanelli thought that his appearance helped his credibility considerably.

He was short, bespectacled, balding. He wore a dark suit, white shirt, dark tie. He appeared to be in excellent physical condition.

As Clifton got to the stand, Racanelli glanced at Cotter. He was staring at Clifton, but Racanelli could not read any expression on his face. That only enhanced the concern Racanelli had been harboring ever since Cotter had not attacked the DNA findings in pretrial sessions.

Racanelli first established Clifton's impressive credentials, then slowly and deliberately, keeping it as simple as possible, he questioned him about the DNA testing. He had learned long ago that if a jury didn't understand something, it tended to disregard it in its deliberations.

Gradually Racanelli led Clifton into a consideration of the blood sample taken from one of Miller's shoes.

Clifton testified that an adequate sample of blood had been safely transported and carefully examined at the laboratory at Genecodes under strict supervision.

To explain himself better, the diminutive Clifton used charts and slides. He had a low-key style that didn't sound as if he were talking down to people.

His conclusion was: the blood that had been taken "off the shoe found in Raymond Miller's closet was blood from the body of Irmgard Werner." The odds against it not being Werner's blood were 772,123,345 to 1.

When he was finished, Racanelli felt that there was no way Cotter could take his findings apart. Clifton had done very well.

As he usually did, Cotter took a long time to get to Clifton, and as he did, he had a sort of country boy look that made it seem as if he wasn't quite sure what he was doing in a big New York City courtroom.

"Dr. Clifton," he said, "I wonder if you could answer a few questions for me?"

"That's why I'm here."

Racanelli bristled. Clifton should answer directly. Juries didn't like wise guys. More than that, Racanelli sensed a little competitiveness in Clifton. He'd better not try to compete with Cotter—he'd be killed.

Cotter nodded at Clifton's answer.

"Dr. Clifton," Cotter said after a while, "you work in Genecodes in White Plains, correct?"

"Yes."

"Are you an officer in Genecodes?"

"Vice president, head of research and development for the Northeast."

Cotter nodded.

"So you're in a position to know the fiscal makeup of the company?"

"What exactly do you mean?"

Cotter glanced at the jury, a slight smile on his face.

"How much does the company make?"

Some of the jury members smiled.

Racanelli stood up.

"Objection, Your Honor. How is this relevant to anything?"

Cotter spread his arms apart a la Ed Koch.

"I'm just trying to establish some basic fiscal facts. If Mr. Racanelli will bear with me, I'll show it's relevance."

The judge nodded.

"I'll allow it, but do make your point quickly, Mr. Cotter."

Cotter looked up at the judge.

"Your Honor, I will make my point quickly, but not so quickly as to damage my case. A man's life is on the line here."

Judge Skolnick looked annoyed.

"I know what's at stake. Proceed, Counselor."

Cotter looked at Clifton.

"So, how much?" he said.

"About two hundred and seventy-eight million."

"That's gross?"

"Yes."

"How much was earmarked for law enforcement studies?"

"What do you mean?"

"How much income did Genecodes make doing tests for law enforcement agencies?"

"We don't break it down."

"I'm not asking you to give me pennies. Just a round number."

"Maybe two hundred and thirty million."

"What was the rest for?"

"Paternity suits and sundry other things."

Cotter paused. He waited until all eyes in the court were riveted on him. Then he spoke.

"So the vast bulk of your income is from cops?"

Cotter paused, Clifton said nothing. Racanelli watched carefully. Cotter had something.

"And how important is it to your company?"

Racanelli was on his feet.

"Your Honor," he said, "this requires speculation on

the part of the witness—and I still don't know quite where Mr. Cotter's going with all this."

"Objection sustained."

"Well," Cotter said, "I think it would be fair to say that two hundred and thirty million out of two hundred and eighty is very important."

Cotter stopped, looked at Clifton.

"And do you know, sir, what percentage of times your tests support prosecutorial goals?"

"Not exactly."

"I see," Cotter said, "but *I* happen to know," and he went back to the defense table and picked up a slip of paper.

"It's ninety-nine point nine percent of the time."

Racanelli was on his feet.

"Objection! Mr. Cotter is clearly implying that Genecodes has a bias for law enforcement. It doesn't. That's just the way tests turn out."

"Sustained."

"Your Honor, I was not trying to persuade anybody of anything. I'm just trying to lay out the facts and let the jury interpret them."

"And where is this going?"

Cotter smiled at Racanelli and walked toward the jury.

"There is," Cotter said, "something else the jury should know about Dr. Clifton that may help persuade them that he is, in fact, biased."

Racanelli looked hard at Clifton.

"Where did you work, Dr. Clifton, before you became a first assistant, then chief of research at Genecodes?"

Clifton's voice was a touch reedy when he answered.

"I was deputy medical examiner in Fontana, California."

"I see," Cotter said. "And why did you leave that job, travel all the way across the country, and take a job with Genecodes?"

"Opportunity."

"Yes, I'm sure," Cotter said, "opportunity and escape."

You could hear a pin drop in the court. Racanelli was frozen.

"Isn't it true that you were suspended from your job and criminal charges brought against you?"

Clifton said nothing.

"True?"

"Yes."

"Will you explain the circumstances?"

Clifton didn't—Cotter did.

"Wasn't it because the defense counsel for one Ricardo Perez had learned that you had doctored forensic evidence on behalf of the district attorney . . . in order to stack the odds against Perez?"

"I was never convicted of anything," Clifton hissed, dropping his professional demeanor.

Cotter swung toward Clifton.

"You're splitting hairs," he thundered. "You copped a plea, agreed to resign your position and get out of forensic medicine in California. Isn't that true?"

Clifton said nothing.

"Isn't it?" Cotter asked again, pointing at Clifton, walking toward him. "Answer me! My client's life is on the line here. Isn't it?"

Clifton's head was bowed and the response was soft—but heard by everyone in the room.

"Yes."

"So, then," Cotter said, "there's no way of telling if you are still biased toward law enforcement, particularly when the survival of your company would seem to depend on it."

"We're not biased."

"Right," Cotter said, "and I'm the tooth fairy."

A wave of laughter swept across the court.

"No further questions."

''Redirect?'' Judge Skolnick said to Racanelli.

''No, Your Honor.''

Later, as he gathered his papers to leave court, Racanelli sensed he was being watched by Raymond Miller, Jr. His blue eyes were flat, amused, and Racanelli thought he saw a quiet glint of triumph.

CHAPTER 56

At around eleven o'clock that night, Racanelli, Lawless, and Racanelli's ADA on the trial with him, Muccio, were sitting in Racanelli's office, trying to assess the damage that Cotter had done to the case that day.

Racanelli was standing at the window, looking out toward Joyce Kilmer Park. A light snow was falling, and everything was white and quiet, the streets empty.

Finally he turned and glanced at Lawless, who was sitting in a chair to the left of the desk, and Muccio, who was sitting to the right.

His voice was low, intense.

''I don't think we're going to help ourselves,'' he said, ''by sweeping today under the rug. Cotter's cross was devastatingly effective, probably fatal.''

''I don't know,'' Muccio said, ''who can tell what a jury will do?''

Racanelli nodded. He liked Muccio. She had self-confidence, her own opinions.

''I realize that, too,'' Racanelli said, ''but I want to operate on a worst case scenario.''

Muccio nodded.

Again there was a silence, then Racanelli said to Lawless: "So your feeling is that his wife knows something, but she's not saying?"

"That's right. What—or how useful—I don't know."

"The thing that struck me," Racanelli said, "is that for all her life she's lived here in New York—and suddenly she moves to Chicago. Doesn't it seem to you that she was burning her bridges, leaving nothing behind that could lead to her?"

"She'd know how to do it," Lawless said, "being married to a cop. I almost didn't find her."

"You're saying that she fled?" Muccio said.

"Yes," Racanelli said.

"No question she was afraid," Lawless said.

"Why?" Racanelli asked. "I would love to get her on the stand and find out why."

"Maybe we should subpoena her."

"I don't think we have enough time. Cotter wouldn't stand for it."

There was a silence; you cold almost hear the gears turning in Racanelli's mind. He remembered something his father had once said.

"The test of a good craftsman, Onofrio," he had said when Racanelli was eleven or twelve years old, "is how well he can get out of the problems that occur on the job."

Racanelli blinked.

"I have an idea," he said, "that might give us a shot. But it depends just as much on what I can do as what you can do, Muccio."

"Do tell."

Three hours later, Ono Racanelli was sitting in the economy-class section of an American Airlines DC 10 as it lifted through the snow at LaGuardia Airport.

The plane banked and turned, and all he could see out of the window was rivulets of water on the glass, a gray whiteness just beyond the wing.

They said the weather was clear for Chicago. He hoped it would stay clear—and that New York would clear up, too.

Chapter 57

It was McKenna who put the plan together for Capezzi, at Capezzi's suggestion—and for an extra three large. . . .

Capezzi figured that if he was making a plan to whack another wise guy, he should make the plans himself: he knew their habits, the kind of people he was dealing with.

But McKenna would know more about cop habits than he did.

McKenna laid the heart of the plan out when they met the morning following the dumping of the renderings on his lawn, a job that Capezzi was going to have to pay thousands to have cleaned up. They met in a diner in Philly, because every now and then an errant wind would waft the stench of the renderings into the house. It had made the house basically uninhabitable. Indeed, some people who lived in the nearby row houses had to get out as well.

"The thing is to isolate these guys. You don't want to try to take them down together. In the first place, you're dealing with bona fide crazies who will not go down without a fight. Number two, when they're together, they can cover each other—and they're four times more dangerous then they would be alone."

"So we take 'em on one at a time," Capezzi said. "Which one first?"

"It doesn't matter. As long as he's alone."

"If we get one, though, the other's going to know the first is missing. He might go underground."

"I don't think either of these guys will go underground. Once whoever's left finds the other's missing, he's going to come looking for you."

"Maybe we could set a trap."

"I have some ideas on just that," McKenna said. "Maybe you'll like them."

"I like what you said already."

They worked out a plan, but they still had a major problem.

Now, since the latest trick—and more than ever—Stein and Piccolo would be alert to being followed or watched. McKenna hadn't seen any evidence of that, but he had to assume it.

The question, then, was how were they going to watch them—to see when they weren't together—without being seen themselves.

McKenna came up with a simple solution, and the next day he did it.

He identified himself to the superintendent of the building on Bainbridge Avenue that was across the street from where Piccolo and Stein lived. He said he was a cop and needed a place to set up surveillance on some suspected drug dealers.

The super bought the story, particularly when McKenna greased his palm with a hundred-dollar bill.

The super set up McKenna in a third-floor apartment directly across the street from Frankenstein's house.

To put the plan in motion, McKenna first called the Five Three and found out that Piccolo and Stein were on four to midnight. That meant that they didn't have to start the surveillance until eight in the morning. McKenna figured they would go to bed sometime in the wee hours and eight would be the earliest they would be up.

The plan to make the snatch was simple. A couple of Capezzi's goons would be parked two blocks up Bainbridge in a van and would talk with McKenna by walkie-talkie. McKenna would watch, and if he saw a good opportunity—one of them alone—he would radio the goons to close in.

There was, he emphasized, no talking with either man. Just action. Giving either of those psychos any opportunity to talk was to give them a warning. That would be dangerous.

Ten minutes after he got into the apartment, McKenna was sitting by the window, watching the entrance to Frankenstein's building.

Chapter 58

Chicago's weather, Racanelli knew, could be characterized as almost balmy. It was twenty-eight, clear, and with very little wind. A lot milder than when Lawless had been out there.

Norma Miller lived on Chicago's South Side at 220 Mayfair Street. Racanelli hailed a cab, and when the driver expressed a reluctance to go there, Racanelli figured it must be a rough neighborhood. He wondered why she'd moved out of a nice home in Brooklyn to live in a Chicago slum. There had to be a reason.

Mayfair Street reflected the driver's concerns. It consisted of a series of battered row houses and garbage-strewn streets. Up the block he saw a wiry dog pass under a streetlight.

There were a few dim street lights, but some of the entrances to the homes were darkened. The street seemed empty, but someone could be lurking in one or more of the doorways. It was hard to tell.

Racanelli climbed the three concrete steps to 220, then let himself into a small foyer that smelled faintly of urine. An overhead bulb cast a dim light. There was a bank of ten mailboxes, only five names were showing. Lutwiniak—or Miller—was not one of them.

Fortunately he knew she was in Apartment 3.

The inside door, which was half metal and half heavy glass reinforced with wire, was closed, but he opened it easily with a plastic credit card.

Inside, the urine smell was even stronger.

Directly ahead was a long flight of stairs. To the side of the stairs was a darkened hall that he assumed led to other apartments.

He climbed the stairs slowly. He hoped the doors had numbers.

When he got to the top, he saw that they did. Apartments 3 and 4 were side by side; Apartment 3 was opposite the stairs. The red doors were chipped and battered.

He stepped quietly up to the door and put his ear against it.

At first he thought he heard people talking inside, but then he realized the TV was on.

It was two-thirty in the morning. She was either still up or had fallen asleep watching TV.

He pushed the doorbell. For a moment he heard nothing; then he heard tentative footsteps coming toward the door.

"Yes?" The voice was low, strained.

"My name is Racanelli. I'm district attorney of the Bronx. I'd like to speak with you about a case I'm on that involves your husband."

"I don't want to talk. Go away."

Racanelli said nothing; then the anger boiled over.

"Listen, lady. You can stay behind that door, but I promise you this. I'll go to the local police station and have a judge fax a subpoena from New York—in which case you'll return with me to New York or go to jail. It's your choice!"

The door opened a couple of inches. There was a chain on it. Norma Miller nee Lutwiniak looked out, then closed the door, removed the chain, and opened it again. "Come in."

Racanelli stepped inside.

CHAPTER 59

At around ten in the morning—two days after they set up the surveillance—McKenna spotted Stein alone. Stein and Piccolo had returned from a twelve-to-eight at about nine.

Immediately he got on the walkie-talkie.

"The big guy just came out of the building alone. He's walking in your direction. Move, but don't do anything until I say so."

Two and a half blocks away McKenna saw the van moving in the direction Stein was walking.

McKenna knew there were three goons in the van. If they got a shot at this guy, they'd better make it good.

The van was almost parallel with Stein when he turned and went into a superette on the corner.

"You see him?" McKenna said.

"Yeah," one of the goons inside the van answered.

"Wait until he comes out. Then coldcock him from behind, got it?"

"Yeah."

Five minutes later, Stein emerged from the superette and started walking back toward his building. Two of the goons were on the corner, and McKenna saw him glance at them as he went by. He thought the glance lingered, but was relieved when Stein continued on his way.

The goons were big and quick.

When Stein was ten feet behind them, they both pulled baseball bats from long coats; Stein was just turning as one of the goons smashed the bat against the side of his head. He dropped his package, and stuff spilled out on the sidewalk.

But he only went halfway down himself, his knees buckling—and then the other goon hit him again, and he went all the way down. McKenna just hoped he wasn't dead—part of the plan was that one of them be taken alive.

The van made a squealing U, and just as a couple of pedestrians became aware of what was going on, Stein, his face a mass of blood that had dripped down from the top of his head, was dumped into the back of the van. The doors were closed, and the van sped off.

"How is he?" McKenna barked into the walkie-talkie.

"Alive," one of the goons replied.

"Okay, use cuffs on him. Don't whack him again."

Chapter 60

When they had gotten home, Piccolo had immediately fed his pets, and Stein, who had run out of San Pellegrino, went down to the corner superette, who stocked it especially for him, to get some. Then Piccolo had turned the tube on—he knew his pets liked to watch, too—and sat down on the couch, lit a cigarette, and used the remote control to turn on a game show.

He didn't really much care for the game show, but he did dig the pretty babes who they used to display all the furniture and other shit they gave away. Some of the contestants were well put together, too.

He sometimes wondered about that Bob Bartlett. That old fuck probably had all the pussy he could handle.

He had been watching the show for about fifteen minutes when he suddenly realized Howie wasn't back yet. He'd just gone for water, so where was he?

He got up from the couch and looked out one of the windows that fronted on Bainbridge Avenue. Then he opened it up and looked out quickly—it was cold and the snakes didn't like the cold—and glanced down the block toward Los Amigos Superette.

Howie was nowhere in sight.

Piccolo debated with himself a moment.

He was, he thought, getting a little crazy. He worried too much. Howie would be back in a few minutes.

Yeah. He put on a short black leather coat and left the apartment.

The street looked empty, and he could feel the tenseness building as he walked toward the superette.

The superette was medium-sized, with two cashiers up-front.

There were only a few people in the store.

Piccolo checked the aisles, Howie wasn't there.

Then he went over to Tony, the store manager, who was talking to the produce guy.

Tony knew Frankenstein—they both shopped there regularly.

"Hey, Frank," Tony said as Piccolo came up to him.

"See my partner?"

"Yeah."

"Where is he?"

"I don't know. He was in about fifteen minutes ago. Got something and left."

"You're sure?" Piccolo asked. A vague fear was starting to gnaw at him.

"Yeah."

"Did you see which way he headed when he left the store?"

"No, I didn't notice. Maybe Felicia did. She waited on him."

Piccolo and Tony went over to Felicia, a dark-eyed Puerto Rican girl.

Tony asked her if she knew who he was talking about. She did, but she didn't notice which way he went when he left the store, either.

Piccolo thanked them and left.

As he climbed the stairs, he felt the tension building.

Something was wrong. This wasn't like Howie. What the fuck was going on?

The call came two hours later.

Piccolo had been chain-smoking and had worked his way through a quart of guinea red.

He picked up on the first ring.

"How you doin'?"

He knew the voice, and a fist gripped his stomach.

"Who's this?"

"You know who it is, Frank."

Piccolo said nothing.

"Where's your partner?" Capezzi said. Piccolo could hear laughter in the background. Piccolo said nothing.

"I want to see you," he said. "We got things to talk about. Go outside, right now, to the corner of Bainbridge and 196th, to the public phone, and wait for it to ring."

* * *

The phone rang ten minutes after Piccolo got to it.

"Okay," Capezzi said, "we got him. If you want to keep him alive—and yourself—you got to do certain things. I want you to head down toward here. You know where *here* is, right?"

"Yeah."

"Call this number at two o'clock."

He gave him a number with a 215 area code.

"Then you'll get other instructions."

"But—"

Piccolo was speaking into a dial tone.

Ten seconds later, an old lady passed by the booth Piccolo was in and stopped.

"You okay, mister?" she asked.

Piccolo nodded. He couldn't speak. He was crying.

CHAPTER 61

Piccolo was back in his apartment, sitting on the couch, his eyes closed, smoking.

He knew Capezzi did not want to talk about anything. He knew that he wanted him to suffer, and then he would kill Howie, and kill him. They would be with the Ferret. . . .

It was, Piccolo thought, all his fault. It was—

He stopped himself. He could not go down that fucking road. He had to help Howie. Oh Jesus, he had to help Howie. They had Howie now, and they were hurting him.

And he knew that if Howie was finished, then so was he.

He had to do something.

Maybe he was dead already. No. No. No. No. No.

He could go to Philadelphia, arm himself to the teeth, blow all those motherfuckers away.

But they would be ready for him. They would blow him and Howie away.

Maybe he could trade himself for Howie.

No, that was crazy. Capezzi would never do that. He wanted both their asses.

Maybe he could call the Philly cops, have them come in.

Why? Who knew how many Capezzi had on the pad. Even if they had the greatest swat team in the world, Capezzi would have Howie so well hidden they wouldn't find him. And once Capezzi found out the cops were coming, that would be the end of Howie.

He took a deep drag on his cigarette and held most of the smoke in.

He closed his eyes. Assuming he hadn't done something already.

Then, suddenly, Piccolo was calm.

It was, he knew, a stage he often reached when stress was high. Inside, it was a feeling that he could do anything; more importantly that he *would* do anything. Anything to save Howie.

It was his edge, the only edge he had, but it was significant. . . .

And then he had an idea.

He went into the bedroom and opened the top drawer of a night table that Howie used.

Thank God Howie was organized. Piccolo found the book instantly, leafed through it.

He found Johnson's number right away.

He dialed the number. It rang once.

"Johnson."

"How you doing?" Piccolo said. "This is Howie Stein's partner, Frank Piccolo."

"Yeah. How you doin'?"

"Listen, Howie asked me to call you. We need another favor."

"Shoot."

CHAPTER 62

The house Piccolo was going to was in Cold Spring Harbor, a posh town on the North Shore of Long Island.

He took the Long Island Expressway, a six-lane highway that ran east and west across the island, and arrived in Cold Spring in about twenty-three minutes, averaging about eighty miles an hour, threading his way through other cars on the expressway like a halfback on a broken field run.

Fortunately he was not picked up by any blue-and-whites.

He stopped at a gas station near the expressway, and an old guy working there told him how to get to the address Johnson had given him.

It was only five minutes away, and he found it without any problem.

The house was on a broad tree-lined street; it was a big white house with pillars. It looked as if it had half a golf course in front of it and, even now, in winter, the lawn was in good shape.

There were two cars in an asphalt driveway that ran to a two-car garage, a small green Spider and a white Eldorado.

Piccolo thought that it didn't matter if she was home as long as someone was in.

He drove around the block, came back and parked on the street a few houses down.

He got out. He was dressed in a black suit and peaked

cap, the same uniform he wore when he and Howie hired the big limo to hit the dealers in Siberia.

He went up a big brick path that wound through the lawn to the massive front door.

He rang the bell.

He stood pleasantly, unthreateningly, and within ten seconds could tell that someone was scoping him from one of the side windows.

A few seconds later the front door opened.

It was a man, maybe thirty-seven. Her husband?

"Yeah?" the man said.

Piccolo glanced down at a notebook.

"Is Ms. Longo here?"

"Why?"

"Well, Mr. Capezzi had a message for her I was supposed to deliver."

"I can take it."

"I'm sorry," Piccolo said, "I have to deliver it only to her."

The man hesitated, then called:

"Maria!"

Frank Piccolo kicked the man in the balls, stepped into the house, and pulled out a .44 Magnum he had shoved down into his pants.

Piccolo made the call ten minutes later from a roadside phone off the Long Island Expressway.

"Yeah?" Aldo said.

"This is Frank Piccolo. I got to speak to Capezzi."

"You're calling early."

"There's a reason."

"What?"

"I'm going to kill his daughter Maria if I don't hear from him in five minutes. Here's the number: 516-555-7757. Got that? Tell him to call me right back."

And he repeated the number and hung up.

Two minutes later, it rang. Piccolo picked up.

"This is Capezzi. What about my daughter?"

"I want to speak with Howie."

"He can't come to the phone."

"You kill him?"

"No."

"Listen up, pig dung. I got your daughter Maria, the one named after the fucking boat that we sent to the fucking bottom of the fucking river. Her fat wop ass is in the trunk of my car. Now if Howie don't come to the phone, I butt fuck her, then kill her, then I make plans to kill all your motherfucking grandchildren. *Capiche*, motherfucker?"

It was said low, fast. It was the scariest moment of Capezzi's life. He had no doubt that Piccolo was speaking the truth. He was nuts.

"Don't hurt her!" His voice was high, placating.

"That's up to you, pig fucker."

"We'll get him."

It took a long time. Piccolo waited. Howie had to be alive.

He heard movement. Then:

"Frank?" The voice was low, hurting. *But there*.

Tears filled Piccolo's eyes, but he kept the feeling out of his voice.

"How you doin', buddy?"

"I'm okay. They gave me a trimming, but I'm okay."

"I'm going to get you out. Hang on. I got his dago dropping . . . his daughter Maria. We're going to arrange a trade. Maria for you. Put him back on. I'll be there, buddy."

But Piccolo knew Capezzi was on, listening on an extension.

"What exactly do you want?"

"A life for a life," Piccolo said. "Howie for Maria."

There was silence.

Piccolo screamed into the phone.

"Don't hesitate, motherfucker. I'll hang this motherfucking phone up and kill everything in this life that matters to you, you pig motherfucker!"

"All right! All right! I'll do it."

"Okay, you wait by the phone for my call."

"Can you answer me one question? Why you break my stones?"

"You killed our friend."

"The snitch?"

"Yeah."

There was a silence.

"I know you're wondering how we could get so worked up over a snitch. It's not something you would understand."

And Piccolo hung up.

CHAPTER 63

Racanelli's suspicion about Norma Miller, nee Lutwiniak, was correct. She was running from Miller, and she explained why. After hearing what she had to say, Racanelli was able to convince her to come to New York to testify. And for one reason:

"If you don't, and he gets off," Racanelli said, "I think you know that your life could be in danger. We found you. So could he."

And to sweeten it, he was able to offer expenses and a fee—three thousand dollars—for doing it.

When American Airlines Flight 768 took off from O'Hare

Airport at six A.M. Chicago time, Norma Miller was sitting beside him.

The plane touched down at LaGuardia Airport at seven-thirty New York time.

Racanelli immediately took a cab to his office and shortly thereafter, Norma Miller was set up in a safe house in the city. He warned the detectives assigned to baby-sit her that she might try to take off.

"Watch her closely," he cautioned. She might ultimately figure that if she did testify—and Miller walked—she could be in real danger.

And there was the question of fear itself. She was terrified of Miller.

Still, even if she tried to testify, there was another hurdle: Cotter. She would be a surprise witness, and Racanelli knew Cotter would fight like hell to keep her off the stand.

At around eight o'clock, Racanelli showered and shaved—and then made a quick stop at Our Lady Queen of Sorrows.

He needed all the help he could get.

CHAPTER 64

As he had anticipated, Cotter fought hard against the appearance of Miller's wife, but in the end the judge ruled in Racanelli's favor.

At exactly 11:01, Norma Miller was called to the stand. Racanelli had no doubt that whatever chance his case had, it was riding on her.

As she walked down the aisle toward the witness stand,

Racanelli watched her. Her eyes searched the crowd and then fixed on Miller, who was sitting at the defense table. Even from his position at the prosecutor's table, Racanelli could see her eyes flash with fear. But, then, quickly she forced herself not to look directly at Miller. Racanelli relaxed.

She was sworn in and, as gently as he could, he brought her through her direct testimony.

Once he had established that she was Miller's ex-wife, where she lived, and other details, he dropped the bomb.

"Why did you leave New York, Norma?"

"I was afraid."

"Afraid of what?"

"Ray."

"You're referring to your husband, Raymond Miller, Jr."

"Yes."

Racanelli paused just a heartbeat.

"Why were you afraid?"

"I didn't want him to kill me, like he did the other one."

Cotter was up on his feet.

"Objection, Your Honor. This is outrageous. There's no proof that Ray Miller wanted to hurt anyone."

"Your Honor," Racanelli said, "I'm just trying to establish why Norma Miller fled—"

"Objection!"

"Sustained."

"Why Norma Miller left New York for Chicago."

The judge hesitated a moment.

"Okay, I'll allow it. Proceed."

"So," Racanelli said, "what made you afraid of your husband?"

"I heard him talking to Spano."

"You refer," Racanelli said, "to Vincent Spano, the person at Social Services that Irmgard Werner reported to?"

"Yes. I knew he worked for Welfare."

"Tell us what you heard."

"I heard them talking about Werner. That Ray was going to do her . . . and they were talking about her insurance. I couldn't hear it all."

"What did you take 'do her' to mean?"

"Kill her."

"Why did you suspect this?"

"I know him. Ray. He could do it."

Cotter was on his feet, the judge chided Norma Miller.

"Mrs. Miller, please confine your response to the questions. Don't speculate about anything you don't know."

"He killed before," Norma Miller said. "Once when he was plastered he told me he murdered his commanding officer in Vietnam. That it was easy, made him feel good."

Cotter on his feet again, whining objections that the judge sustained—but the jury had heard what Miller said.

"So," Racanelli said, "you specifically feared for your life."

"A couple of days after I heard them mention this woman, I saw a little item in the paper about her being dead. I figured if life meant so little to Ray, he might just set me up, too. I had life insurance."

Again, Cotter was on his feet, red-faced, objecting.

Five minutes later, Racanelli was finished eliciting direct testimony from Norma Miller.

Then Cotter rose and started the cross-examination.

Racanelli held his breath.

Cotter was at the top of his whining, dramatic best. He went at Norma Miller with nothing short of savagery; though he had a style that made it seem as if he were being as considerate as possible, he practically gutted the witness.

Racanelli thought she stood up quite well, at least in relating the facts as she saw them.

But Cotter was able to bring out that Racanelli was paying her three thousand dollars for her testimony. He and Cotter went round and round about that, Racanelli stating—as he knew Cotter knew—that it was a normal procedure in certain instances, that is was just an extension of the witness protection program run by the government.

Of course, Cotter claimed that it really was buying the allegiance of a witness. "Pay some people three thousand dollars and they'll jump through a flaming hoop for you," Cotter stated, generating slight smiles from some members of the jury.

After almost two hours, Cotter completed his cross of Norma Miller. Racanelli hoped the jury noticed that she avoided looking into the eyes of Raymond Miller as she passed the defense table.

Overall, Racanelli thought she'd done well. Depending on what Miller presented, and his final statement to the jury, he had a very good shot.

Chapter 65

Final arguments, as it happened, were on a Monday, and the prosecutor, as was the custom, presented his summation first.

In some cases, the summation was icing on the cake; in this case, Racanelli felt, it was the cake. If he could put it together well, and with fire, he could win—assuming Cotter didn't have a great day.

Racanelli did not have to refer to his notes to make his summation. The case was part of him.

At 10:01 he got up from the defense table and approached the jury box. He was conservatively dressed, as usual, in a dark blue suit, white shirt, plain tie. The blue suit was a tradition. He had been wearing a blue suit during final arguments ever since he had first begun as an ADA many years earlier.

He started to speak in that low, measured way he had and immediately launched into his main theme: circumstantial evidence.

''Ladies and gentlemen,'' he said, ''movies and television and fictional books have somehow created an impression in the minds of many that circumstantial evidence is not strong evidence. But the contrary is true. Circumstantial evidence, viewed collectively, is very strong evidence—because it can lead to a logical, inevitable conclusion. If, for example, you owned a puppy and left him alone one day, and when you came home the stuffing had been pulled out of the couch, and maybe the puppy was hiding under the bed, what would you conclude? You did not see the puppy attack the couch, but you have the clear circumstantial evidence that he did. Logic would lead you to the conclusion that the puppy was the perpetrator.''

A number of the jurors smiled.

''In this case we also have the equivalent of a ruined couch, and it must lead to the inevitable conclusion of Raymond Miller's guilt. Let me review the evidence.''

Piece by piece, Racanelli spoke about the evidence: the Corvette that Miller and Irmgard were spotted in, the kid in the 7-Eleven remembering Miller coming in, the matching handwriting on the money orders, the pubic hair, the blood on the shoe, the calls Irmgard made to Bloom, the calls between Irmgard and Spano . . .

Then he spoke about motive.

''Norma Miller's flight from Miller helps us to understand what kind of man he is—and she also gave us a motive. The motive of a man with a heart of stone, a machine that has no more caring for other people than he does for a rock.

"She told us why Miller killed—and would kill again. He killed for money, greed, and then he calculatedly killed his coconspirator, Spano.

"I know that Mr. Cotter will tell you that none of this is proven. And I will freely admit that it is not. But I ask you this: Isn't it a reasonable explanation given the circumstantial evidence, given the statements of Norma Miller?

"I would add, too, that you don't even need to have the motive for murder. What you have is enough. A chain of evidence that clearly points to Raymond Miller. . . ."

Racanelli had been standing in front of the jury and speaking directly to them. Now he turned and walked slowly toward Miller. As he did, Miller looked at him with his bland, flat blue eyes. The last eyes, Racanelli thought, that Irmgard had ever looked into. The eyes of a murderer. He suddenly felt enraged.

"One thing we have not spoken about during this trial," Racanelli said, looking down at Miller, "is that Raymond Miller is more than just a murderer. He is also a police officer, someone who has sworn to uphold the law, who has promised to protect us from criminals.

"But he violated that trust, too, in the most heinous way possible."

Racanelli gathered himself for his final statement.

"Irmgard Werner believed in him, too. She also trusted him. You saw the results of that trust in the forensic photos you were shown.

"I knew Irmgard Werner. She had had a hard and desperate existence, but she was on her way back to a better life—and she thought that the man sitting at that table would help lead her to it."

Racanelli smiled sardonically.

"Now all that she has left, all that we can give her, is justice. Show her that it doesn't matter that she lived in a welfare hotel, lived on the fringes of society. Show her that she mattered—that her life mattered—because under the law she is equal. A guilty verdict will prove all this to her . . . I thank you.

Cotter followed with his statement, and he had a great day.

He walked back in forth in front of the jury, his arms outstretched, his voice cajoling, his face a mask of disbelief.

"I would agree with Mr. Racanelli that circumstantial evidence is strong evidence. But the point," Cotter said, pausing to look directly at the jury, "is that it has to be *good quality circumstantial evidence.*"

Cotter then proceeded to remind the jurors how he had vitiated the *particular* evidence that Racanelli had presented.

"What he's left with is a cute story about a puppy. It's adorable—but it hasn't got *bubkus* to do with this particular trial."

Then, finally, he launched into an attack on Norma Miller—and reaffirmed why he believed she was testifying against Raymond Miller.

"Money. Three thousand dollars is why! If I could have that kind of money to work with, I could get people to fly in from Chicago for a day, too! That's fifteen thousand dollars a week! When's the next plane leaving?"

That got a good laugh.

Cotter then thanked the jury for its patience and attention and sat down.

The following morning Judge Skolnick charged the jury. Racanelli did not feel it favored either the defense or the prosecution. It just outlined the law, and cautioned the jury about keeping their deliberations to themselves.

Then they retired to consider a verdict.

As they filed out, Racanelli turned and looked toward the spectators. Rebecca Werner had sat in the same spot every day the trial was on.

Racanelli smiled at her, and she smiled back.

CHAPTER 66

Piccolo crossed the Walt Whitman Bridge, though in his mind he was in Pleiku, in a snake-and-spider-infested tunnel crawling with VC. In other words, in his element.

The plan had been fairly easy to formulate.

First he had considered contacting Lawless and other squad members. He knew that Capezzi would try to take him and Howie out—that was the main goal—and he knew that Lawless and the squad guys would go with him.

But that wouldn't have been fair. If there was any shooting, people would get clipped, and he didn't want that to happen to anybody else. And even if they just whacked the goons, there would still be hell to pay. Yeah, even if no one was shot, it wouldn't matter once precinct bigwigs found out. Siberia wasn't much, but it was something. Anybody caught would be thrown off the job, maybe face criminal charges.

So he decided against it. It didn't matter, though. He knew he had an edge, no matter how many goons Capezzi had. His edge was that he was willing to die to set Howie free. With concern for his life no concern, it opened up all kinds of possibilities for plans.

He decided on one quickly, and he figured that the only thing he had to be concerned about was the beginning. Once he had it set up, he didn't need to worry. If they whacked him outright, then that was it, too. But then Capezzi would be minus one daughter.

When he had called Capezzi, he had been told to meet at Capezzi's trailer on Penrose, that the exchange could take place there, if that was okay.

Capezzi said he wanted to be "clean." He would play straight, if Frank would play straight.

In other words, don't bring any company.

As he drove along the Schuylkill Expressway, he glanced into the rearview mirror, and though he couldn't see anything, he spoke.

"How you doin' back there, honey?"

"Please," Maria Longo said, "where are you taking me?"

"Back to your father. We're going to make a trade. You for my partner Howie. You think your father will get cute?"

She started to sob.

"Why you crying? Think maybe your father will try to fuck me and you'll die, right?"

Piccolo paused, then spoke again.

"I don't think he will, Maria. Everything's going to be peachy keen."

They drove for another five minutes.

"We're almost there," Piccolo said. "Time to get ready."

With that, he pulled into a diner, threaded his way toward the back of the place.

Capezzi was sitting behind the desk in the trailer, eating a pepperoni pizza.

He was nervous, but no one around him knew. No one around him ever saw what he was feeling—except for anger. They could tell that by his actions and his voice, which got high, and when he spoke in Italian.

What made him nervous was that he was dealing with a psycho. This fucker might try to clip Maria, him, do anything. He was a fucking nut.

He was due to show up in five minutes.

Capezzi tried to predict what he'd do.

Maybe he'd bring an army of cops.

Capezzi didn't think so. This was a guy who would come by himself.

They would make the exchange cleanly. Then they would see.

Chapter 67

Piccolo was ready by the time he turned his Trans Am onto Penrose Street. Maria Longo was now in the front passenger seat next to him.

The street looked empty, except for the usual wrecks, assorted pickups, and regular cars parked outside the junkyards that lined the street.

But he knew he was being watched.

There were plenty of places, mostly trailers, where Capezzi could set up a sniper to whack him. But Piccolo wasn't really that worried.

He pulled up in front of the trailer and parked about ten yards away from the front entrance.

He didn't need to beep his horn. Magically, one of Capezzi's goons, Aldo, emerged.

He went over to the car. His face was white and grim.

"How you doin', ace?" Piccolo said. "You tell Capezzi what we got going on here. And tell him I want to see Howie soon."

The goon disappeared into the trailer.

Inside Capezzi was standing up.

"Mr. Capezzi," Aldo said, "he wants you to come out. He's got Maria there . . . He's got tape around her neck that's taped to his wrist and a gun in his hand. Jesus, Mr. Capezzi, the muzzle's flush against her head."

"Madre de dios."

Capezzi went outside. He approached the car. It was true.

"Papa," Maria cried, "Papa."

He held up a hand.

"Where's my fucking partner?" Piccolo said.

Capezzi looked into his eyes. The look made him fart.

He turned, motioned to Aldo, who was standing in the doorway.

"He'll be here in a minute."

"That's fucking nice," Piccolo said. "And, hey, Maria, shut the fuck up. Stop crying. You're pissing me off."

And he laughed. It coated the inside of Capezzi's belly with frost. He tried not to look at the gun.

Fifteen seconds later, a van came down the block and stopped in front of the trailer.

"What now?" Capezzi said.

"Howie's in there?"

"Yes."

"You are going to drive the van down the block. We make the exchange there."

If Capezzi had thought of hesitating, he did not.

"All right."

The driver got out of the van, and Capezzi, with difficulty, climbed up into the van, which was still running.

A moment later the van was moving down the block.

Piccolo gunned the Trans Am past it and stopped at the corner.

In his mind, this was the moment: he was deep in the tunnel.

He stayed in the car. Capezzi sat in the van.

''Get out!'' Piccolo yelled.

Capezzi got out.

''Open up the van and let him out.''

Capezzi went to the back of the van and opened first one door, then another. Piccolo watched.

Howie came to the back of the truck. His face was swollen, his hands cuffed behind his back.

Piccolo almost lost it.

''Motherfucker!'' he screamed. ''Motherfucker!''

''I'm okay, Frank,'' Howie said. He had gotten out of the van and was standing on the street.

''Get out, cunt,'' Piccolo said.

Maria Longo's hands were free. She opened the door. She got out slowly and carefully.

Then they were on the street.

''Take the cuffs off,'' Piccolo said.

Capezzi reached into his pocket and, with shaking hands, succeeded in getting the cuffs off.

''Howie, get the wheel.''

Howie went around and got behind the wheel.

Capezzi looked at Piccolo.

''What about my daughter?''

So fast that Capezzi hardly saw it, Piccolo took out a banana knife, flicked it open, and sliced the duct-tape harness that bound him to Maria Longo.

Then just as quickly the knife was gone and a .44 Magnum was in its place.

''I should empty this in your balls,'' Piccolo said. ''Maybe someday you'll give me another chance.''

Then he was in the Trans Am, and Howie was gunning it away.

Capezzi watched them go, his terror rapidly changing to rage.

CHAPTER 68

Every prosecutor hopes that a jury will deliberate all of an hour or so and then return with a guilty verdict. In other words, they shouldn't agonize over it.

Sometimes, of course, this is the case; most of the time, it is not. Being the member of a jury is, for most people, a responsibility taken seriously, particularly in cases involving capital crimes.

The jury in the Miller case had received the case in the afternoon at about three P.M. Two days later, they had not yet reached a verdict.

Racanelli was worried, but he knew Cotter was worried, too. There was just no way to tell what the deliberations meant.

So far, the jury had not called for any readbacks, so there was no way to even get a hint of what was going on in their minds.

Becky Werner said that she would stay around for the verdict.

"Whatever happens," she told Racanelli, who took her to lunch the second day of jury deliberations, "I want to thank you for caring about Mother. There's some sort of comfort knowing that she just didn't die and was forgotten about."

For Racanelli, it was not enough, though. He needed a guilty verdict. Raymond Miller was a cold-blooded killer. If he got away with this, there would always be something missing, something not right. This was America, a place where anyone could get equal justice under the law. It was something that his father had taught him since he was a little boy, and he still believed that to be true.

It happened like most things really good or bad in life—unexpectedly.

The third day of jury deliberations, just as Racanelli was about to go to lunch, he got the call.

"The jury's coming back with a verdict," the court clerk told him.

Twenty minutes later, everyone was assembled, and the jury foreman, a heavyset man who worked for the Sanitation Department, stood up.

"Have you reached a verdict?" Judge Skolnick asked.

"Yes, we have, Your Honor."

"And what is it?"

"Guilty."

Racanelli swallowed hard. His assistant, Muccio, shook his hand. He looked across at the defense table and found himself looking into the eyes of Raymond Miller, Jr. The eyes reflected neither blandness nor triumph now but rage; at that moment Racanelli was sure if Miller could kill him, he would.

And then Racanelli turned toward the spectators, looked at Becky Werner. She was dabbing her eyes. She waved to him. All was right with the world.

CHAPTER 69

Five minutes after they sped away from Penrose Street, Frankenstein made a stop at the marina on the Schuylkill River, where they had sunk Capezzi's boat and where, of course, the Ferret's body had been dumped.

Both men walked to the edge of the river and looked down. The water was dark, murky.

They had come to pay their last respects to August "the Ferret" Rondolpho.

And, they also knew, take on McKenna and a shooter who were going to try to whack them.

Frankenstein spotted the cars at the same time. As Capezzi had driven the van to the end of the block, two cars had appeared, one two blocks away, and the other in the opposite direction, a block away. In other words, there was no way Frankenstein could get off Penrose without one of the cars—if they were goon cars—being able to follow them.

And Frankenstein had no doubt they were. One was a gray Toyota, the one McKenna owned.

When Howie had driven off Penrose, he had taken the route past McKenna's car on purpose, and as they passed they got a glimpse of him in the driver's seat.

Now, the gray car had stopped about seventy-five yards away, its nose just peeking out from beyond the corner of a building.

They waited, saying nothing, standing casually, as if they didn't have a care in the world.

Then the car started to move toward them.

Piccolo said:

"Don't fire until you see the whites of their fucking eyes."

The car started to gather speed.

They were within forty yards when Piccolo said:

"Let's do it to it!"

Then they suddenly whirled, and out came the hardware, Stein with a fourteen-shot Baretta that Piccolo had given him in the car and Piccolo with a .44 Magnum, the world's biggest handgun which, in the little man's hand, looked like a small cannon.

They both fired from a modified Weaver stance, and Stein had gotten off three shots and Piccolo one before McKenna could take any evasive action.

Then, suddenly, the windshield shattered and the car started to careen, tires screaming, and Frankenstein kept firing. Frankenstein screamed as they fired, and McKenna never even had a chance to lean out the window and do his thing before the car started to swerve to the right, toward the river. Then, just like in the movies, the car went up on two wheels, on its side, and they kept firing. It went hurtling off the dock, for a moment suspended in midair, Frankenstein still firing, then belly flopped in the river raising a great splash.

Frankenstein ran toward the river and were just in time to see it go under all the way. They caught a glimpse of McKenna in the front seat; it looked as if someone had doused him with ketchup.

Then the car sank beneath the surface. Gurgle. Gurgle.

They waited thirty seconds. It was obvious that no one was going to come up.

They bolted for their car, the second shooter, in the second car, having taken off during their little skirmish with McKenna, and soon the scene was history.

As they drove away, they thought similar thoughts:

How appropriate that McKenna should join the Ferret in the Schuylkill—how ironic; and, most of all, how sweet!

CHAPTER 70

Two months after Raymond Miller was convicted of second-degree murder, Judge Ira Skolnick lived up to his reputation as being the only Jewish descendant of Judge Roy Bean.

He delivered a vituperative tongue-lashing as he sentenced Raymond Miller to the maximum of twenty-five-to-life and said he only regretted that the death penalty was not still on the books; though Miller would be eligible for parole after having served eighteen years, the judge was going to put in a strong recommendation that he serve the full sentence of life and be denied parole.

"You are really guilty of first-degree murder," Skolnick said, "and were only tried for second-degree because of the constraints of the law. Killers don't come any more malignant than you, Miller."

The sentence suited Ono Racanelli and Joe Lawless just fine. And they both knew that as an ex-cop Miller would have his hands full in whatever upstate psycho house he would be residing.

Three weeks after the one-way shootout at the marina, Frankenstein returned to Philadelphia and the Schuylkill River to finish paying their respects to the Ferret. They did it at night, so they could also pay their respects to McKenna by urinating in the river.

They had not noticed anyone following them since that day, and both men felt it unlikely that anyone would.

A few hours after the shootout, they had called Capezzi, told him of McKenna's demise, and warned him but good.

"If anyone tries to clip us," Piccolo, serving as spokesperson, had said, "they better succeed. Any attempt will be treated most severely. In other words, we will kill every living thing that belongs to you, and we will get you. Got it, Jabba?"

Capezzi had not answered, but they were sure he got it. And they knew he must be wondering just what they would do next. Maybe they'd decide to whack him. At least they hoped he would think that.

Now, they looked into the water, which reflected the light of the moon.

"Hey, Frank, now everything's complete. The stars have been put back in their proper order. You know what I mean?"

And Piccolo did. He understood completely.

"Fuckin' A," he replied.

About the Author

Tom Philbin is the son and grandson of cops. His previous *Precinct: Siberia* novels are PRECINCT: SIBERIA, UNDER COVER, COP KILLER, A MATTER OF DEGREE, JAMAICA KILL, STREET KILLER, and DEATH SENTENCE. He lives on Long Island.